SALEEMA ISHQ

SISTERS ARCANA

A THRILLER

ISBN: 979-8-9916057-1-7 (Paperback)

Cover design by: Miblart

Published by: Fearless Phrases Publishing LLC

Sisters Arcana

PROLOGUE

In the quiet moments, I can still see the wet curls clinging to her neck while the gentle waves of the Rio Grande tug at the salt cedar wrapped around her calf, unwilling to let go. I remember sucking in a sharp breath and choking on the scent of grief hanging in the air.

Even before seeing her lifeless body, I knew she was gone. That's the thing about gut feelings – they surface before we can make sense of them. It began as a subtle vibration deep within my gut, growing with each passing moment until finally transforming into a full-blown quake. My insides clench at the visceral memory, causing me to double over and claw at the remnants of the past still lingering in my core.

We look to our gut for messages, just as seers often experience an intuitive ache based on nothing more than a quick glance at a tarot card, rune, or a person's palm. But that's the powerful thing about intuition. Even with the traditional meanings behind these signs or symbols, each reading is open to interpretation based on the gut feeling.

The Devil card generally has nothing to do with demons, while symbols for death don't necessarily mean imminent death. Instead, they can be interpreted as *transformation* or as an *end* — and, therefore, a new beginning.

In one moment, her full rosebud lips were animated with laughter, and in the next, they'd turned blue, her final breath still lingering by the time I reached her. Yet I already knew, for her, there was no other interpretation for Death.

CHAPTER 1

(NOW)

As my eyes trace the maze of numbers and equations on my computer screen, a sense of calm washes over me. They're like a balm for my turbulent thoughts. I take a long sip of lavender tea and lean in closer, eager to solve the mathematical problem before me. Others might think mathematical modeling is a mundane life path, but to me it's like painting a masterpiece with logic. I get to explore endless possibilities, while confidently leaning on the fact that math will always follow strict rules. And as someone who grapples with the overwhelming uncertainties of life, rules are my solace.

That's why on Friday afternoons, like today, I carry my chair to the other edge of my double-sided desk in my home office and sit facing the picture window. It's my reward for reaching the end of the week. From here, I can see the family of roadrunners dart from their home in the arroyo through my yard, their speckled crest feathers glistening in the sun. The meadowlarks perched on the fence serenade me with melodic trills. But it's the hummingbirds that steal my heart. The meager two feeders I moved in with have grown to nearly twenty, and likewise, my charm of iridescent hummers has grown.

A flash of red catches my attention, tearing my gaze away from my monitor just in time to welcome Blaze. She's the latest addition to the entourage, though she blends in with the rest of the flock as if she's been part of it forever. Blaze is easy to pick out with her scarlet throat feathers that glisten blood red in the sun. Her appearance reminds me to pull my shoulders back and lift my ribcage, exuding an air of confidence that's eluded me longer than I'd like to admit. If only navigating the human existence were as graceful as a hummingbird's movements. My thirty years have been anything but graceful.

I could marvel at my shimmery friends for hours, their delicate beaks dipping in and out of the nectar while hovering inches away from the windowpane. And that's precisely why I enacted the rule to only face this direction on Fridays from 2 pm to 5 pm.

My home office is small and modest, but it's my sanctuary. The only place where I feel like I can be my true self. The walls are lined with bookshelves adorned with my books neatly organized by book size and color rather than genre or author. This system is much more appealing than the ones libraries and bookstores employ. I have 1,072 books on these shelves, and I know where each and every one lives.

My gaze drifts from the vibrant emerald of Blaze's beating wings and wanders along the bookshelves toward the green section. I spot the spine of *The Inheritance Games*, and a smile creeps across my lips. *I knew it. A perfect match.*

I'm nearly startled out of my chair by the sound of the doorbell. A quick glance at the calendar confirms what I already know: I'm not expecting a package to be delivered until next Thursday between 11 am and 3 pm.

My hands tighten the bathrobe tie around my waist — wearing it is another Friday rule — and I trod across the hardwood floor to peer through the peephole. I see a small child who can't be much older than six or seven years old. Definitely too young to be without a parent, yet I don't see anyone else. I place my hands on my hips and glance back at my beckoning office. My numbers and hummers will have to wait a few moments.

"Just a minute!" I shout through the door, though I know it'll take me more than just one. Because of the increasing crime in my neighborhood, slight as it may be, I've installed two extra locks in addition to my standard two. *Four locks. Four. Four fours are sixteen. Sixteen sixteens are two hundred and fifty-six.* My eyes instinctively squeeze shut, and I rapidly rattle my head back and forth as the numbers coat my gray matter. *Just breathe. It's only a child.*

By the time I get the door open, the little girl has inched her way to the far edge of my hacienda-style portal. She fingers a translucent purple clipboard loaded with cookie brochures – the child's wide eyes remain fixed on my face. I do my best to unfurrow my brow and smile, but she still looks like she's seen a ghost. I get that look a lot, but usually not until people have gotten to know me first.

"Can I help you?" I peer around the door, careful not to pass the threshold.

"Mhmm."

"Well, what is it?" I reply with more urgency, catching the abrasive edge to my voice. I try not to become impatient with this quiet little thing because she reminds me so much of *her.* The thought causes a tug in my throat, and I realize that's precisely how I used to act. Maybe not at her age, maybe not until after the incident. After that, my self-awareness and confidence were absolutely crushed.

"Was there something you wanted to ask me?" I try again with a little more compassion and even crouch down to bring myself to her level. "Maybe something about cookies?"

Her gaze softens slightly, but she still doesn't speak.

Two hours and seventeen minutes left in my work day. One hundred and thirty-seven minutes. Eight thousand, two hundred and twenty seconds. The longer I'm here, the less time I can spend with my beloved hummingbirds.

"Well, then—" I stand quickly and glance beyond the girl down my flagstone path, then along the cracked sidewalk in front of my home. "Where are your parents?"

She twists her tiny body and points to an idling Lexus across the street. I cross my arms, eyes darting between the car and the small child. *Please don't get out of the car.* The invisible barrier at my front door feels more present than ever. *Please, please don't ask me to walk over there.* The sound of my heartbeat fills the silence while my shoulders begin to ache from the unease. After what feels like an eternity but is likely only ten seconds, my silent prayers are answered.

"I have to get back to work," I shout at the heavily tinted car windows, then shoot the girl a quick glance as I turn on my heels and return to my sealed fortress. After securing the locks, a wave of guilt washes over me, though it lasts only a moment. The little girl's presence has disrupted the rhythm of my carefully scheduled day, and as I walk back to my office, I feel my breath quicken. Each inhalation and exhale mirror my racing thoughts.

I settle into my chair and watch as Blaze playfully dances and dives with another hummer, yet I still can't catch my breath. I need my numbers to soothe my soul.

"Alright, if x is greater than one, according to the Lorenz System, then y would be proportional to the square root of ϱ minus one." I allow myself to become absorbed in my world of equations. My respirations gradually normalize as the ball of tension in my chest slackens. The deeper I delve, the laxer it becomes, though it isn't entirely released. It remains fastened to a dark place in my core. Still, the symphony of bird chirps and key clicks pulls me from my spiral of anxiety, bit by bit, number by number.

The doorbell chimes again and the numbers in my mind scatter like startled hummingbirds. I let out an exasperated sigh and rapidly shake my head as if the movement will realign the figures. The shaking intensifies as the idea of ignoring the bell creeps into my mind. It's likely just the little girl again. The odds that a person would ring my doorbell twice in one afternoon are approximately 31.6%. *Thirty-one point six. Nine hundred and ninety-eight point fifty-six.*

When I reach the door, I check the peephole, expecting to see the familiar sight of the purple clipboard. But no one is there. Even when I slowly open the door a few inches and peer out, my eyes narrowed with suspicion, the street is hauntingly empty. I spot the back of the Lexus turning down the block, signaling that the little girl and their not-so-involved guardian must have given up and moved on to the next neighborhood.

See? I roll my eyes with a sheepish grin. *All that worry for nothing. You can trust the numbers, Aisha,* I remind myself.

I start to close the door when a flash of red grabs my attention. A red piece of paper is wedged in the weather stripping. I pluck it out and examine it, but it's not just a piece of paper. It's an envelope, though it has no stamp and no return address. Just "AISHA" written on the front.

I scan the area again, feeling the hairs on the back of my neck stand up. *Is someone watching me right now?* After a careful search reveals nothing, I replace the locks with trembling hands, then lean against the closed door. My heart thuds against my ribs. I take a deep breath and remind myself that this is just another problem to solve, though the sense of dread hovering over me suggests it's one that should have been addressed long ago.

CHAPTER 2

(NOW)

AFTER EIGHT LONG minutes of pacing around my office, I still have the envelope clenched between my fingers. *Eight by eight is sixty-four. Sixty-four, sixty-four, sixty-four.* I can tell the cardstock is expensive. It's thick and weighty, as if secrets were woven into the material instead of silk fibers. Like the kind someone would use for a wedding invitation. Or a funeral announcement.

My thumb grazes over my name on the front. Not even my mail comes to Aisha Wren. I'm A. Wren to the outside world. Clearly whoever sent this knows me.

What if I just don't open it? I could simply drop it into the trash and return to my perfectly planned life. But the card would remain there, taunting me from the trash bin. I wouldn't be able to concentrate. *What if its looming presence distracts me so deeply that I use the wrong value for a variable in my work and calculate an incorrect outcome?* I could lose my job. Then, I'd lose my beloved house. I'd end up on the street. The cascade of thoughts causes my body temperature to rise. No, I can't ignore it and risk everything. There's only one practical option: open it now, then figure out a course of action.

With a determined nod, I tear into the envelope. A single card lies within. The edges are aged and weathered from time and use. One side features a delicate mandala pattern in emerald greens. I flip it over, and a chill courses through me.

An illustrated image of a figure suspended upside down stares back at me. The figure's limbs are contorted as if caught in some unseen trap. Along with the disturbing image is a handwritten message: "Within the sway of The Hanged Man's silhouette, a friend from a past life beckons. A memory hung in the shadows yet to be revealed."

What the actual eff? A surge of alarm passes through me.

I flip the card over again and again, fervently examining both sides. The symmetry of the backside brings me a sense of calm, while the disturbing image on the front forces my stomach to flip. Still, I can't look away.

A quick internet search confirms that it's a tarot card: The Hanged Man. But what's even more unsettling than the image itself is there appears to be no fixed or even universally agreed upon meaning for the card, or any tarot card for that matter. How can tarot have absolutely no rules?

My foot taps against the leg of my ergonomic chair as I swiftly scroll through the search engine results. There are plenty of articles, videos, blog posts, and forums with explanations for beginners, but I'm looking for something more specific. My mouse stops as soon as I spot a video titled "What Are the Rules of Tarot? Q&A with Lumaara."

Bingo.

"Grand rising, beautiful light beings, and welcome back to my channel," the YouTuber says in a breathy voice that's as light as the feathers hanging from her ears. Her delicate hands flow through the air while she speaks, as if conducting an invisible orchestra. "Today we're answering a few of my most frequently asked questions, including what tarot is, all about the rules, and how you can begin using it to awaken your intuition." She motions above her head while I suppress an eye roll.

"Tarot is a divination tool involving a deck of seventy-eight cards to support you and your highest self. Each card or group of cards, referred to as a spread, can provide you with insight into your past, present, or future. Magical, isn't it?"

I don't disagree, but I need to understand how the cards work and what The Hanged Man means. Just one of seventy-eight cards. *Seventy-eight by seventy-eight is six thousand and eighty-four.*

I shift in my seat and open my desk drawer that contains my neatly arranged assortment of office supplies. I reach behind the stacks of vibrant Post-it notes and pens, sorted by color and width, and flip through a plethora of notebooks. Each one is labeled: Daily Tasks, Budget & Financials, Brainstorms, Dream Journal, Mathematical Theorems, Hummingbirds, and at least a half dozen more. Notes on tarot cards don't seem to fall into any of the categories. Brainstorms are probably the most appropriate. I slide the matte olive book out of its place and flip to the next blank page, readying my favorite pen for note taking.

"While each card has an individual meaning," Lumaara goes on, "there are really no rules when reading tarot. You consider the energy associated with the card and the context rather than simply following what the card says. That's the beauty of this sacred art." She winks at the camera. "Make sure you give this video a thumbs up and follow me o—"

"This isn't art, it's chaos!" I slam my pen down on my journal, and then slump backward into my chair and stare at the card. The cryptic words gnaw at me. Who could this "friend from a past life" refer to? And what memories do they hold? I can count my friends, both past and present, on one hand. When your life is as regimented as mine, it's difficult to make plans with people. Spontaneous outings won't do, and most people in their late twenties to mid-thirties aren't willing to book a meetup four weeks in advance. So, while I have lost touch with acquaintances, I wouldn't say any of them were ever true friends.

The anxiety rises from my chest into my throat as the patterns and equations that typically bring me solace swirl around in my mind like a twister – with so much speed that each immediately slips from my grasp. I'm reminded that I wasn't always this way. There was a time before my schedules when my life blossomed with spontaneity. When I enjoyed the company of not just one but four best friends. Sisters. But those days are long gone. I shake my head in an attempt to push the memories from my mind, then begin jotting down a plan.

I need answers, and I know precisely who I should reach out to, but I'm petrified at the thought of reopening wounds. Wounds *I* inflicted.

Especially after all this time.

CHAPTER 3

(THEN)

My legs move as fast as I can make them go in the deep, soft sand of the arroyo. It feels like running through peanut butter — not that I've ever done that, but I definitely would if I could. Peanut butter is my absolute favorite food. I could eat it for every single meal, which is why it's such a bummer that Mom won't let me have more than three spoonfuls a day. "Any more and you'll turn into peanut butter!" she says.

I yell a joke about how my peanut butter fears are finally coming true. Through the cloud of dust behind my big sissy, I can tell she likes it. She snorts and gasps until we both fall into a big pile of giggles. The sand spills into my favorite sneakers and digs itself under my fingernails, but I don't care. This arroyo is my favorite place in the whole entire world. My playground for all my eleven years. It just sucks that we can only play here from the time the final bell rings in June until the first day of the new school year.

When the three other girls finally catch up, their frowns don't match the smiles we wear. "Aisha!" they shriek in unison. "You were supposed to let us win!" Lulu's high-pitched voice drills right through my head and I instinctively cup my hands into earmuffs.

"I guess I changed my mind!" I throw my shoulders up toward my frizzy, lopsided pigtails, then notice Lulu's nose turning as pink as her Barbie bedspread. Big tears sprout on her lower lashes and threaten to tumble down her cheeks. Before I can say a word, Noora steps in.

"It's OK, Lu. We don't always have to win." Noora's voice is gentle and soothing. She takes her role as big sister very seriously, and she really is everything you could want in one. Instead of just leading with her heart, like Mom says I do, she leads with her heart *and* her head. I should probably try to do that a little bit more, but probably not 'til I'm more grown up. Maybe when I'm Noora's age in like six years.

Lulu dramatically wipes away her tears with the back of her tiny fists. "I just don't like losing," she whispers through sniffles.

"Oh, we know," I add. In response, Lulu scrunches her nose and sticks out her tongue at me.

"Hey, Sissies!" I turn toward the distant voice and see Kayla and Marie have gone on ahead and are waving from the abandoned tree house deep in the arroyo. They're not our real sisters, but we're all so close that it basically feels like we are. The two of them have lived down the street from us for as long as I can remember, so we practically grew up together. Sleepovers always include all five of us. Family trips mean it's the Wrens *and* the Perezes. Marie finally started joining us on more adventures this year because she finally turned six, but we still keep a close eye on her because she's so small for her age. I love my sissies more than anything — all of them.

Kayla and Marie scurry up the weathered old wood, and even though they're both pretty small, the old wood looks like it could come tumbling down at any second. Noora lets out a gasp as Marie's foot slips on the ladder. The nervousness radiates off of her with almost as much force as the hot sun beating down on my face.

"Sissy!" I call toward the tree house before Noora can yell out a warning about safety. Sometimes I think she worries too much. She'll lecture us about how we could fall and get hurt and break our limbs and stuff. Sure, that did happen to someone in the grade above me last year while fooling around on the playground equipment in the middle school yard, but that's not going to happen to us. We're careful. Plus, worrying is Mom's job, not Noora's. A big sister is supposed to teach you how to French braid your hair and prank call boys, like they do in the movies. But I get it. I do feel protective over Lulu sometimes, but more than anything, she's just kind of annoying. I guess that's a little sister's job.

Marie steadies herself and calls back, "I'm OK, Noora!"

"Go keep an eye on them, please." Noora says it under her breath, and I expect her voice to go up at the end, something I just learned in English class indicates a question, but it doesn't really sound like a question from Noora. It's more of a command.

"Fine." I cross my arms and pop my right hip out, a new pose I discovered that makes me look just like Mandy Moore on the cover of *J-14* magazine. "But I'm only going because I want to play up there, too," I say. "Not because I think they need watching." Then off I go toward the rickety house.

"Thanks, Aish," I hear from behind me.

My feet glide right up the ladder without so much as a wobble. I duck under the peeling paint of the small doorway and breath in the stale air of the tree house. I kinda like the smell. It has so many happy memories attached to it. We discovered the abandoned tree house two summers ago and it basically became the basis of our Sissy relationship. We play here any chance we get and use it as our hideaway whenever anyone has anything important to discuss.

Like when Kayla and Marie's parents almost got divorced. They didn't really understand what that meant, so we tried to explain things the best we could. Because, like our family, theirs barely talks about feelings. I tried my best to be there for Kayla during that time. I'd whisk her away to the bathroom between class periods before the other kids had a chance to see her runny nose and puffy eyes, then we'd meet in the tree house after school where she could finally give in to the sadness. I'd hold her shaking body, all the while wondering what it was like to have two parents. But I figured that having one who was always there might be better than having two who fought all the time.

My eyes adjust to the low light of the glorified wooden box we've claimed as our own until I can make out two figures who wave me over. They're seated in the corner of the tree house, alongside all the cobwebs and dust bunnies.

"Whatcha doing, Sissies?" I join them and plunk down onto the rough wood. The entire house shudders and Kayla and Marie place their hands on the floor of the house as if it'll steady us, but there's really no point. If the tree house is going to come down, it'll come down. And one day it definitely will.

"Just looking at our spell book," Kayla replies. A single ray of sunlight shines through some broken slats in the roof of the house, and that's where they've placed the book. She flips through the pages that are so shiny Kayla's face looks like it's glowing. It's a bit creepy, if I'm being honest. Her big wide grin and glowing teeth make her look like a witch. Our spell book isn't that kind of book, though. It's more about fairy magic and using the Earth to cast spells for good. Definitely not evil. We wouldn't mess with that stuff.

Our book doesn't even look like a spell book. Not like the ones you see in *Charmed* or *Sabrina the Teenage Witch* or our other favorite shows. This one looks brand spanking new with its glossy cover and totally white pages. Kayla and I found it at the Scholastic Book Fair last year and knew we had to have it. But it cost way more than what either of our parents gave us to spend at the fair, so the sissies all pooled our money and bought it. It now lives in the tree house in three separate zip lock baggies to keep it dry and clean. Not that it rains here in New Mexico all that much, but, like Mom says, "It happens when you least expect it."

"Awesome sauce!" I reply, then immediately feel my body fold inward from embarrassment. Kayla and Marie look at each other and burst out laughing. Of course I join them because it is actually really funny. I've been trying out different slang recently. I'm not sure this one is quite me, but I'll never know unless I try! I lean forward and look at the page Kayla has open: "Fluttering Heart Charm to Catch Your Crush's Eye."

"That's not the one you want to try today, is it?" I ask with one eyebrow raised. Kayla's face flushes until it's almost the same color as the red Tamagotchi hanging off her belt loop. I notice Marie's eyes narrow as she looks up at Kayla.

"I keep saying we should do the Friendship E-licker, bu—"

"It's Elixir, Marie!" Kayla rolls her eyes and jumps to her feet. "And I told you we're not doing that one."

I glance over at Marie and her sad eyes find the floor. But Kayla doesn't seem to notice. "I'm going to grab some juniper berries for the spell!" She beams, then leaps out the doorway and fumbles down the ladder.

"C'mon, let's go," I tell Marie, grabbing the book. I shove it between my chest and my chin as I climb down the ladder, careful not to miss a step. Going up is so much easier than coming back down.

As soon as I feel my feet hit the hot sand, I clutch the book in my hands and look up toward Marie. She's as white as a ghost and perfectly still.

"C'mon, you need to come down." She doesn't budge.

"Kayla always holds me when I do it," she finally says.

I whip my head around and spot Kayla at the opposite bank of the arroyo, scrounging around for juniper.

"Well, she's not here right now, so I'm all you've got," I say. Marie bends over and carefully grabs hold of the side of the ladder, then begins to lower her legs down. She's so tiny, her toes barely even touch the next step. The only way she'll make it is if she jumps. I carefully place the book on the sand.

"Sissy," I call, "you need to jump."

She looks down at me then back up toward the tree house. Ground. Tree house. Again. And again.

"C'mon, you'll be fine," I say again, doing my best to give her a big, confident smile. *Channel Noora, heart and head. Heart and head.* She nods, then carefully removes one foot and then the other until she's just dangling there from her hands. I brace my legs underneath me and reach my arms toward Marie.

"It's OK, I've got you," I shout upward. "You can let go."

CHAPTER 4

(NOW)

"THE HANGED MAN card is all about letting go."

I'm propped on the arm of my reading chair scrolling through Instagram Reels featuring the breathy tarot woman. Sitting square in the cozy chair doesn't feel quite appropriate, since I'm not actually reading, although neither does standing. Who am I kidding — nothing about this feels right.

I force my eyes to focus on the phone screen. Despite her haphazard bohemian style setup with mirror-studded pillows strewn all over the ground and crystals hanging behind her at random intervals, she seems to know what she's talking about. And I would hope so, considering she has over 172,000 followers on this platform alone. *One hundred and seventy-two; twenty-nine thousand, five hundred and eighty-four.* Better.

"Is there something in your life that's in need of surrender?

Grand rising, beautiful light beings. I'm Lumaara and today we'll explore the mysterious Hanged Man card." The YouTube video I watched earlier must have been rather old, because Lumaara's hair now reaches her waist — a mane of bouncy, dark curls twisting every which way. The last time I tried to wear my hair down like hers, it did the exact same thing. I wear it in a neat bun every day except Fridays, which are my days to let loose. Today it's in a French braid.

"If you're intimidated by The Hanged Man, don't be."

"Easy for you to say," I groan as I glance at the card propped up against my desk organizer. "You didn't just have one eerily dropped off at your doorstep."

"When this card appears, it's a sign that you're stuck. Maybe not physically, but it's possible you're in a rut and your current lifestyle simply isn't aligned with where you want to be because you're fighting against yourself." Lumaara pauses and leans into the camera, her intense gaze bores through me.

"Does this sound like you?"

I shift on the armrest, the words throwing me off balance. It's as if she's speaking directly to me. The words echo in my head, bringing forth an image of my daily routine laid out in front of me. But instead of feeling reassured and safe, I suddenly feel constricted by my boundaries, like a ring worn on a hot, humid day. A metallic taste lingers on my tongue and I take a sip of the now lukewarm lavender tea.

"The interesting thing about The Hanged Man is that most believe he's in that position by choice." *Who would willingly put themselves in such an uncomfortable position?* I shudder at the thought and wrap my free arm around my body, feeling the warmth of my fingertips through my linen romper.

"This card urges us to see things from a different perspective. To stop swimming upstream. Surrender to the process.

Let go, light beings." The video fades into ambient music and soft musings as Lumaara guides her viewers through a meditation designed to help with releasing whatever it is that is meant to fall away. But my mind has already drifted back to the card. The mandala-like pattern. The contorted limbs of The Hanged Man.

There's only one person who would know how this card relates to me and my life. They might know who this friend from a past life could be. I pull up the Facebook app on my phone to jog my memory for potential connections. My fingers scroll past the "People You May Know" section, which is essentially code for "People You Definitely Know But Have No Desire to Connect With." I roll my eyes as I recognize an old crush from college, my boss, and Aunt Patsy.

But then, a new notion hits the spiral of thoughts in my head and sends them flying. This person I'm considering might not just know who it is, *they might actually be the friend from a past life.*

My thumbs pound the screen of my iPhone and open the Instagram app. Suddenly a swirl of new thoughts emerge. Will she even remember me? Most likely, but will she want to hear from me? *What if she's as reluctant to connect with me as I am with her?* The worries sprout roots and extend deep into my mind as quickly as the hummingbirds come flocking to my window when I fill up their feeders.

The movements of my fingers slow as I grapple with these what ifs and questions, yet I continue searching for the profile I'm determined to locate. It's not hard, because I was just watching her Reels.

I scroll to the top of the profile, then stop short as I consider what I should say. I could start with a generic salutation. "I hope this message finds you well" or "Long time no talk!

How have you been?"

"No, way, way too awkward," I mumble as my gaze finds the ceiling in the hopes that the perfect message might be etched on the inside of my skull. Maybe I'll just get right to the point with something like "So… I found this creepy tarot card at my front door and wondered if you sent it or know who did?" Naw, too accusatory.

After several minutes of staring at the screen and calculating which message would have the most positive outcome, I put my fingers to work. I've settled on five words. Five short yet powerful words. *Five fives are twenty-five, six hundred and twenty-five.* Lumaara's bright smile and effortless glow stare back at me in the squares on her Instagram profile. I hit the Message button, type it out, then press send without giving myself time to overthink it.

@Algebrainiac_A.Wren_: Hey sis, can we talk?

CHAPTER 5

(THEN)

WITH MARIE SAFELY on solid ground, I use a stick to write my name and Noora's in the soft arroyo sand in big loopy letters, then "Sissies 4 Eva." Lulu grabs the stick and starts scrawling out something. At first, I think it is Kayla's name, but it just keeps going and going and going.

"Whatcha writin', Lu?" I peer over her shoulder and try to sound it out.

"Ka-munk-i-or?"

She shakes her little head in big, dramatic motions. Lulu doesn't do anything small.

"No! It's Kamonkeeyore!" I stare at her, waiting for an explanation, but she has a satisfied smile on her face as she turns back to jamming her stick into the ground.

The wind picks up and blows bits of sand over the writing

and up into her waist-long mane. And it's literally a mane. I keep telling her that she needs to be Simba for Halloween, but she's not as excited about the idea as I am. If my hair was as long and wavy as hers, I'd definitely do it. Instead, I have these wild curls that never look the same way twice, but whatever.

"Kamonk what?" I ask.

"It's my new name."

"Oh yeah?"

She stares up at me with her enormous eyes. Mom said she'd grow into them eventually, but they still look way too big for her face.

"Well, I like it," I say as I squeeze her shoulder. "But I also really like your real name."

Lulu's mouth starts to curve into a frown, and I can see her whole body deflate. My little sister has never been a fan of her name, although I don't really understand why. "Lulu" is so cute, like the name of a kitten or a floofy puppy. Which might be why she hates it so much. Because Lulu *is* cute, just like a kitten or floofy puppy.

Even though she can be so annoying sometimes, I still want to squeeze her round cheeks and pet her long, soft hair whenever I see her. As I rest both of my hands on her shoulders and look down onto her unbelievably long eyelashes, I want to do just that. Instead, I kneel down on the warm sand and give her a hug. She leans into me and rests her head on my shoulder like she does with Noora, and little flowers of joy seem to bloom where our skin connects. But our moment is interrupted by a gust of warm wind that sweeps over, around, and between us, nearly knocking little Lu over.

"Remember, it means 'pearl' in Arabic," I say. I try to catch Lulu's eye but she won't lift her gaze. Her eyes stay fixed on the ground.

"And Maaji says pearls mean wisdom, Lu." We stay quiet for a few minutes, listening to the soft buzz of cicadas and the cottonwood leaves rustling in the breeze.

"I know," she finally says. "And I *am* wise."

I wasn't expecting *that* after such a long and heavy silence, but I'm not *not* happy to hear it.

"You totally are!" I confirm.

She nods her head in agreement. Big. Dramatic. Nods.

"That's why I like having different names and different forms."

I lift my eyebrows. OK, another really unexpected reply. By now the other girls have heard whispers of our conversation and come over to where we are, kneeling in the sand.

"Um, what?" Noora asks, her perfect, dark eyebrow arched up high. I can tell she's worrying again.

"You know, a different form." Lulu stares at us like we should know exactly what she's talking about but we just look around at each other.

"Like Sailor Moon!" Marie shouts, spinning around and around, mimicking the way Sailor Moon transforms in the anime.

"Exactly!" Lulu shouts, then joins her.

They spin and spin until they get dizzy and fall in the warm sand, their cackles filling the air with joy. Noora, Kayla, and I look at each other and can't help but giggle.

I give Kayla a little "Wazzup?" nod and she smiles back. I love that we can read each other's minds with just a glance. I can't even do that with my real sissies.

We both jump to our feet and grasp hands — right over left and right over left, just like Jack and Rose do in *Titanic* — then start spinning. I like to think about what it would be like at the front of that enormous ship. I mean, minus what happened in the end, but the whole "standing there with your arms out and feeling the breeze on your face" thing that Rose does sounds like so much fun. I'd do that in a heartbeat.

As Kayla and I spin around, I close my eyes and imagine what it would feel like to be on the ocean like that. I can practically feel it splashing up and hitting my face. Tiny drops of hope on my eyelids and lips. I open my eyes. It's totally raining when I least expected it.

CHAPTER 6

(NOW)

IT TAKES MY sister only five hours to reach me. She's been in Colorado all this time. Colorado! A mere 319 miles away from Rio Erizo. *Three hundred and nineteen squared is one hundred and one thousand, seven hundred and sixty-one.* Yet we may as well have been living on different planets because after eleven years of not seeing each other — since my little sister's high school graduation — we know absolutely nothing about each other. Which is clear, given the fact that she insists on speaking in person rather than on the phone or even FaceTime.

@Algebrainiac_A.Wren_: You really don't have to come all the way here.

I typed furiously into my iPhone as I paced around my house. The kitchen and living room are divided by a half wall, creating a ring-shaped path that my feet instinctively follow whenever I'm deep in thought. Because of the countless laps I've taken here, the hardwood floor is worry-worn in a perfect circle.

@Lumaara333: no, i do! i want to!!!! it'll be so good to see each other.

@Algebrainiac_A.Wren_: My home really isn't ready for guests...

@Lumaara333: i don't care! i'm your sister, silly! if it's that big of a deal i'll find an air bnb nearby.

@Algebrainiac_A.Wren_: No!

@Lumaara333: LOL, ok, no air bnb then...

@Algebrainiac_A.Wren_: You really really don't need to come visit.

@Lumaara333: i insist! this is happening sissy.

Lulu always gets what Lulu wants. I sigh and pause in front of the kitchen sink to gaze out the window. A whiff of basil from my windowsill herb garden finds its way into my nostrils and I breathe deeply, relishing the earthy scent. There's no use fighting with my sister at this point. At least I can control where we meet, which must be my house. There's really no other way.

@Algebrainiac_A.Wren_: Fine, my house it is then. I'll send you my address in a sec.

@Lumaara333: YAY!!! so excited!

And less than a day later, here we are.

"Ishie sissy!" Her voice doesn't have the breathy quality it does in her Instagram or YouTube videos. Instead, it's so shrill it pierces right through my head. Just as I remembered it. But all the soft edges of the cute young woman I last saw are now angled and contoured to boot. Standing in front of me is a woman who could easily be mistaken as a model. Her mane of curls falls over one shoulder like a waterfall of dark silk, while a vibrant, patchwork skirt hugs her waist and hips in all the right places. My gaze lingers on the intricate beadwork of her skirt as I try not to look at her camisole. Not just because it would be rude to stare, but because the color of it sends shivers through my body. It's a deep peacock blue color, almost identical to the color that haunts my dreams.

"Hi Lulu." I keep my hands tight to my sides and dip my head down slightly while bending at the waist, my eyes moving to her face when I straighten back up. *What the eff, Aisha. Did you just bow?* Her doe-like eyes move from one side of me to the other and I realize I'm standing smack dab in the middle of the doorway. It's been a while since I've done this.

"Sorry, come on in. Your shoes can go here." I point to the tidy Target shoe rack by the door. I'd panic-ordered it last night after she responded to my message and said she could be here by morning. But she doesn't need to know that. Or the fact that I haven't had anyone other than my plumber step into my home in the last four years.

"Sure thing," Lulu giggles, booping my nose with a slender, hennaed finger. I watch from my post in the doorway as her thin frame settles onto my couch to remove her woven sandals, then flings them toward the shoe rack. Her rings clank togeth-er as she rises to wander the room, fingers running along the wall and up my entertainment center. Above my TV is where I keep my treasured hummingbird collection. I have porcelain figurines, teacups, music boxes, and, of course, books, all featuring my beloved hummers.

"I didn't realize you had such a thing for hummingbirds," Lulu breathes, her eyes fixed on a Swarovski figurine. My entire body stiffens. Not only is this the newest addition to my collection, but it's also the most expensive and most delicate. The hummingbird sits above the crystal lily with only its delicate beak keeping it up. The coil of tension tightens within my spine as she reaches for the gorgeous crystal bird. The pale pink crystal reflects in her thick silver bangles.

"Oh yeah." I feign a laugh and step between the shelf and her eager hand. "I guess there's a lot you don't know about me. Or I about you—"

"I know! Let's change that," Lulu exclaims with wide eyes, then quickly wraps her fingers around my wrist. My skin vibrates at the touch. A gasp escapes my lips but Lulu doesn't notice. She pulls me down toward the couch, and I'm surprised at how strong she is despite her petite size. My body sinks right into the soft material while she remains perched on the cushion like a little bird.

"OK, what did you have in mi—"

"Got a light?" She barely looks up from the mirrored purse she's rifling through. The thought of cigarette smoke billowing through my house forces my teeth to grind together and my tongue to sharpen. Who does she think she is? After all this time and considering I'm the one who invited her back into my life? I cross my arms and sit up tall, ready to unleash a storm of words on her when she pulls out a small piece of wood and an enormous crystal.

"Palo santo," she says in response to my crossed eyebrows, as if I have any clue what that could possibly mean. "It's holy wood."

I shake my head and she tries again.

"For smudging?"

My shoulders rise up.

"Cleansing?"

"I've never he—"

"Burning it can help with spiritual healing, and I thought clearing your space and lighting it before we talk could help with," she uses the piece of wood to motion to herself then me, "us."

Her nose starts to turn a rosy-pink color and I can almost see tears bloom on her lashes. Just above her right eye are those three tiny freckles. *Three threes are nine, nine nines are eighty-one.* Despite the shimmery bronzer and specks of glitter peppering her temples, the freckles look just like they did when we last saw each other. Over a decade ago.

I'd spent all night pacing around my home playing over and over what I expected to happen this morning. How our reunion would go. I'd concocted numerous possibilities, any-where from her running toward me with a knife as soon as I opened the door to her not showing up at all. Each scenario got more and more complex, a host of characters making their ways into my worst case scenario. However, in none of them did I consider how she'd be feeling about our reconnection.

Yet, here she is, talking about "us" and trying not to weep. My heart hurts for my little sister, though not enough to push away the paranoia that keeps creeping into the back of my head.

"I didn't actually DM you to catch up." I squeeze my hands together, my nails digging into the soft flesh of my thumb. Lu-lu's smile immediately falls and her eyes dart around the room then land back on me. Her expression is ice cold.

"I mean, we can certainly do that after," I add quickly, mak-ing eye contact but unable to hold her piercing gaze. "And I did print out a few ice breaker questions just in case. Well, I filled out my answers already, but you ca—"

"Why exactly am I here, Aisha?" Her voice is now neither shrill nor breathy. It drips with judgment and suspicion. *Act fast,* I urge myself. *Before you lose your nerve.*

"I need to ask you about this card." I slip my fingers into the pocket of my romper and place it on the coffee table. The edges are even more worn now because I've had it in my pocket since last night. I really didn't want to keep it close to me, but I was worried I was making this whole thing up and wanted to have it nearby as a reminder that it's real. I've slipped my finger into the pocket just to touch it at least a few hundred times, and each time it sends a shudder through my spine.

Lulu picks up the card, grasping it gingerly by the corner, and lifts it up toward the window. The light doesn't shine through the card; instead, the image on the front glistens. Her eyes narrow and she examines both sides, flipping it over and over again just as I'd done initially. Finally, she places it on the coffee table and grabs my hands in hers. Her stiletto nails dig into my palms. I let out a yelp — not from the piercing in my hands, but from her expression. She has a huge smile on her face and I can see every single one of her blindingly white teeth.

"Aisha, I am so glad you called me about this," Lulu says through her eerie grin. "It's as if the Universe aligned our meeting as perfectly as the pattern on this tarot card."

The pit in my stomach doubles in size as soon as the words escape her lips. What have I done?

CHAPTER 7

(THEN)

THE OTHER GIRLS are going absolutely wild over the rain, dancing around and splashing in the puddles, but not Lulu. She's sitting there on the ground with her legs criss-cross-apple-sauce style staring up at the sky. She has her hands held up in front of her face and closely watches every drop as it falls from the clouds all the way until it splashes into her palm. If I didn't know for sure we have the same parents, I would definitely think we weren't related. She's just so… different.

The last time Mom made a whole chicken for dinner a few years ago, Lulu cried. But it wasn't just regular crying. She was body shaking, snot dripping, "you worry that they're going to cry so hard they barf" crying. She hated seeing the chicken's legs and wings, but worst of all, she hated the idea that we were going to eat another living being.

"Aisha, your dear little sister is a very sensitive soul," Mom said to me as she lay down on my bed next to me. It had taken her almost four hours to get Lulu to settle down and finally fall asleep after dinner.

"Let's do something special for her tomorrow," I suggested.

"That's a beautiful idea." Mom kissed me on my forehead, then stroked the bridge of my nose with her thumb. It felt so good and always put me to sleep, but not that night. After she left, I tossed and turned thinking about how I could make my little sister feel less sad. Luckily, I came up with the best idea.

Mom and I went out early the next day and stocked up on all kinds of vegetarian meat substitutes, like black bean burgers, fake chicken nuggets, and even vegetarian breakfast sausage. I hovered by Lulu's bedroom door until she finally woke up. I couldn't wait to serve her breakfast. But she wasn't nearly as excited.

"I think I want some sausage, Mom," she said over the piles of steaming hot food sitting on the kitchen table.

"It's right here, Lu." I picked up the plate of fake sausage and offered it to her.

"No, real sausage."

"Are you sure, sweetheart?" Mom asked hesitantly. "Even after last night?"

"Yep, I'm OK," she said through slurps of milk. "I'm OK eating animals."

Mom simply shrugged while I sat there in disbelief, my mouth wide open. I'm not sure what she did with all of those strong emotions. She must have stuffed them down into her soul where no one could find them, not even her.

I see glimpses of the deeply feeling younger Lulu sometimes, like now while she stares at the raindrops. I can't even begin to guess what she's thinking about. Maybe something about how Mother Nature is absolutely incredible to make everything so magical and perfect. I've considered that before, but I don't sit on the ground and get quiet about it. Lulu definitely needs quiet.

Noora, on the other hand, always has a knack for picking out the moment when things shift from fun to freaky, which is why she rounds us up as soon as the rain changes from a sprinkle into a light downpour.

"Alright Sissies, let's head home," Noora sighs. She slides the plastic bag-protected spell book into the back of her jeans, grabs Lulu's hand, then makes for the trail. Only Marie protests. Her tears mingle with the rain drops drizzling down her cheeks. I can't hear the tantrum she's making through the rain tappy tapping away, but I can definitely make out her tiny feet stomping into the ground. After a little pep talk from Kayla, the two hug, then we're on our way. We fall into a single file line and follow Noora out of the arroyo, leaving a trail of giggles behind us.

Climbing through the sand is hard enough on a dry day, but the rain makes it that much tougher. Our feet slip around in the soft ground, sending handfuls of the wet grit into our shoes. Mine feel like they weigh about a million tons apiece right about now. Water has already started to pool into our footprints from earlier today. Of course, I can't help but jump in a puddle. Kayla shrieks with delight as the water sprays her already soaked shorts. Her laugh is my very favorite sound.

"Hey!" Noora's voice is right behind me, so close it throws me off balance. I throw my palms out to catch myself, barely missing a cholla. My big sister stands over me with one hand on her hip. "See? I was about to tell you two to quit messing around or you'll get hurt, and look what happens?"

I leap to my feet and point at the black eyeliner running

down her face. "Oh yeah? Well, I'm going to tell Mom you're wearing *waaaaay* more makeup than you're supposed to be!" I jab back.

That definitely grates her cheese because she turns up her nose and turns her back on me without another word. Within a second she's scrambling up the slick slope. Kayla and I scurry after her, grabbing onto the branches of piñon trees on the edge of the trail. We pass all our path markers: the trunk that looks like a little fairy door, the rusty abandoned pickup cab, and the collection of found items of jewelry that have been hung on a cactus like it's a Christmas tree. Each one reminds us that we're getting closer to the top of the trail, until we finally burst through the trees onto the sidewalk of Cactus Creek Lane.

I give Noora a big grin and present my hands, arms, and legs to her Vanna White-style. "Not even a scratch!" I say with pride. But my wisecrack doesn't even register. Noora's too busy looking over and around us at the opening in the trees. She grabs my shoulders and pulls me toward her, staring at me with a look I've never seen before. Before she even opens her mouth I can tell something is very wrong.

"Where are the littles?"

I look to Kayla and see a flash of panic shoot across her face.

"Marie!" Noora calls out. "Lulu?" But no response. For a second, I feel my stomach drop. Like it does when you hit turbulence on an airplane, even though the ground is right under me. We need to find the littles.

CHAPTER 8

(NOW)

I PEEK AROUND the corner into the living room just to make
sure Lulu's still there and hasn't silently snuck out of my home,
but, sure enough, she's in the exact same unwavering position.
A glance at my watch confirms that she's been meditating for
exactly forty-eight minutes. That seems like an awfully long
time.

After burning some of that pungent palo santo, she posi-
tioned herself in the middle of my floor with her legs crossed
and eyes closed. I think using the time to examine the card
would be more useful but she seems to think otherwise.

"I'm going to see if the card has any messages for me," she
explained when I tried to suggest having one of my research
colleagues run it through an image analysis software. "It could
give me some insight into who left it for you or why."

"OK…" I wasn't convinced. Did she have to come all this way just to do that? We were wasting precious time. Almost two hours since she arrived at my doorstep. *Two twos are four, sixteen, two hundred and fifty-six.* My hands were sore from gripping and rubbing them so tightly, but I felt a ball of tension in my pit that wouldn't let up. "I mean, that is the goal, so I guess we should try anything that'll help us get there?" Lulu simply smiled and nodded, then slipped into her meditative state.

On Saturdays between 9 am and 11:15 am, I sit in my fuzzy reading chair and read whatever fiction novel I'm currently devouring. I always have a fiction and a non-fiction book in progress — one to allow my head to float up into the clouds, and the other to keep me grounded. With Lulu meditating, I can finally settle back into my schedule and retain a bit of normalcy. But when I ease into the chair, all I can think about is what she's doing. Is she touching my Swarovski hummingbird? What if she destroys the card without me knowing? I know I'm being completely paranoid but feel it's justified. I haven't seen my sister in so long and feel as though I barely even know her.

I can't see her from my reading chair, so I quietly rise and take a seat at my desk. It feels so unnatural because it's Saturday and I never ever work on Saturdays, but my heart leaps into my throat as I wonder what she's up to. The safety of having her within my eyeline outweighs the discomfort of sitting out of place. I lean my head and shoulders over to the left until I can catch a glimpse of the back of Lulu's head. That'll have to do. I cannot control the fact that I have an Instagram influencer sitting in my living room, but I can control my watch over her. I open my book while maintaining the precarious position and try to read but the words fly out of my head as quickly as they enter my eyes.

Suddenly, Lulu stirs and I hear her breathe in deeply, then exhale in a sort of roar. A smile creeps across my face as I'm reminded of my sister's childhood obsession with lions. Noora always reminded her to channel her inner lion and "lead with courage" when we were kids. It appears my little sister is doing just that, whereas I've turned to leading my life through fear.

She reaches toward the ground with her hands, then un-pretzels her crossed legs and flings them over her torso into a handstand. I gasp, thinking only of my precious hummingbird figurine, which startles Lulu and she tumbles onto the couch.

I attempt to scream but nothing comes out. I'm shackled to my desk. Why can't I move?

My sister springs off the couch as if nothing happened and brushes herself off. "Oh, sorry, I didn't know you were in there," she says cheerily, yet I'm still in shock. Not because of the fall, but because of the way I responded. I haven't been involved in many startling events that left me feeling absolutely petrified lately. Well, not in the last several years. Perhaps not since one of my hummingbirds crashed into my office window and gave me a fright. I'd sat there for several minutes, unsure what I could do or how to proceed. It's as if my heart stopped and time stopped with it. *Oh no, it's happening again.*

"O-Oh, yeah, I'm here," is all I can manage. *Just breathe in, then out.* Lulu's made her way into my office and is peeking at all of my books. She's running her fingers along them, then pulls one off the bookshelf. *Big Magic.* Of course she'd pick that one. It's the exact book I would have chosen for her if she asked for a reading recommendation. But we don't have time to talk books right now.

"So… anything?" I finally move my heavy legs and walk over to her as she thumbs through the pages. I try to resist pulling it from her hands as she bends the pages back a little too far.

"It's a very powerful card." She says it more to herself than as a response to my question. I position my body right in front of hers. I can't bring myself to look at her blue top, so instead, I let my eyes investigate her face. Her forehead and mouth look perfectly relaxed, so much so that they look practically expressionless. Why isn't there any urgency in her explanation? What is she keeping from me?

"OK?" An awkward silence hangs between us. Lulu stares at the book and I stare at her. It feels as though you could cut the tension with a knife. Perhaps she doesn't feel it but I certainly do. So many thoughts run through my mind, but one question pushes itself to the front. It pushes itself up my throat and to the tip of my tongue. I can no longer hold it in.

"Lulu? That's all you're going to give me?" My sister tears her gaze away from the book and I feel it penetrate my soul.

"Well, I have a theory." She tosses the book down on my desk then moves toward my reading chair. I quickly retrieve *Big Magic* and fan through the pages. *Phew, no creases.* I instinctively know exactly where it goes on the shelf, and as I turn around, I notice Lulu curling up in my favorite chair. Her flowy skirt rises as she tucks her knees up toward her chin. I spot a detailed tattoo of a lion on her calf.

"But you're not going to like it," she continues.

"No, Lu. We're not doing that."

"What am I doing?"

"Not communicating," I say.

She responds with a shrug, and I feel my hands clench into fists.

"It may have worked when we were kids as a way to cope with everything that went down, but we're adults now." That was the Wren way. Modesty was less about hiding your body and more about hiding your feelings. They all got swept under the rug as soon as they appeared.

"Just tell me," I demand. The not knowing gnaws at me with each passing moment.

She wraps her hands around her slender shoulders and sits up straight.

"Do you remember that old tire swing?"

I slowly nod as I piece together what she's telling me.

"Well, I think that's the reference to The Hanged Man."

"And the friend?" I'm not sure if I want to even know, but I ask anyway, "Do you think it's…?"

Lulu reaches her hand out and places it on top of mine as she gives me a slow and deliberate nod. A flicker of regret pulses through me from a place deep within. I'm not used to this much touch but I will myself not to flinch. Still, there's a deep longing within me that wants to grab my baby sister and hold her close to me. Breathe in her Herbal Essences shampoo like I did that night by the river. Tell her everything's going to be fine and remind myself of the same. But I don't. Instead, I remain perfectly still until the sound of Lulu's phone alarm shatters the silence.

"Ohmigod, my Live!" She leaps off the chair and frantically scrolls through her phone, continuing without looking up. "I have to prep for this Instagram Live my PR person scheduled for me. I have five minutes. Shit! Five minutes!"

Five fives is twenty-five. Twenty-five twenty-fives is six hundred and twenty-five. I'm left alone in my office with only my swirling thoughts and numbers to keep me company. Back to my natural state. I'd been longing for it all day, but it doesn't feel quite as good as I'd imagined.

CHAPTER 9

(THEN)

I DON'T GET why Noora is freaking out so much, like really freaking out. She always worries, but this is definitely extreme. I remind her that we have absolutely no reason to worry because everything is fine.

"They know to go to our house!" I say as I try to catch up with her past the jewelry cactus and the old truck, moving my heavy feet as fast as they'll go. I've said the same thing over and over since the street, but Noora doesn't seem to hear me. Or maybe she doesn't believe me.

"If we just head home, I'm sure they'll be there," I shout as a warm feeling expands in my chest. *I know I'm right about this.*

"But that doesn't… make any… sense!" Noora pants back. The rain is starting to let up but in its place sits a thick layer of fog.

"Did you see them walk past us?" she adds when she finally has enough oxygen.

My big sister has a point.

"No, but they know that's our meeting place. 'Always meet at home base' is like the first rule of the Sissy Code!" I turn to Kayla for support but she just shrugs at me. She doesn't believe me either?

Noora lifts her head from her bent over, hands-on-knees position and tilts it to the side as if she's thinking about what I just said. Finally. But she then lets her head hang again just as quickly.

"I just hope—" she whispers toward the ground, "I just hope he doesn't find them first." It takes me a few seconds to figure out who she's talking about, but then it hits me. Dr. Wiley. Our parents still haven't told us everything that happened at the neighborhood watch meeting or why we're not allowed near his house anymore. Apparently, they even had the police involved. Kayla and I begged and begged to hear more, but they told us we'd have to wait until we were more grown up, though Kayla overheard her dad say something about "dark voodoo." Noora mentioning him seems to light a fire under both her and Kayla, and they propel down the path, continuing to retrace our steps.

"Marie! Lulu!" They yell in unison as they slide down the soggy ground.

Except I don't follow them. My feet stay planted right where they are. Something inside of me is telling me that I'm right, and when I get that feeling, I know I can trust it. Mom always says something about how a woman's intuition is a super powerful thing. I'm only eleven, so I'm not a woman quite yet, but I will be someday. And why not start practicing now?

They're at home, they've got to be. I know it.

Without another thought, I turn on my heels and race back up to the street. My body feels so light this time, like I'm floating up the hill and barely even touching the ground.

On Cactus Creek Lane I take a sharp left and race down the street. My lungs and legs burn even worse than they do after running the mile in P.E., but I can't stop. Not until I've found the little sissies and prove to Noora that I can handle being responsible. She's not the only big sister in the family. Even though I'm a little sissy to her, I'm still a big sister, too.

Our house comes into view and a smile spreads across my face. *Almost there.* But something pink catches the corner of my eye and makes me stop right in my tracks.

"Lulu!"

Of course, Marie is right on her tail. I let my shoulders fall from where they sit practically up to my ears. *I found the littles all by myself! They're almost home like I thought. But not quite.* When I finally catch up with them, it dawns on me just where we are.

"Lu, Marie," I say in a hushed voice. "Whatcha doing?" Although I know exactly what they're doing.

"Just visiting the tire swing." Lulu's smiling eyes meet mine. They're filled to the brim with pride.

"OK." My eyes scan the vast front yard and street to see if anyone else sees us, but luckily, the coast is clear. "You know we're not allowed to go on it anymore, though." I say it in my best big sister voice, but it still doesn't sound as good as Noora's. Noora! She must still be freaking out worrying about the little sissies. I need to get the girls home safe first, then find Noora to tell her she can stop looking.

"We know." Lulu looks up at me, then points to her feet. "See, we're still on the sidewalk, nowhere near the swing." Both their feet are right up against the green grass of Dr. Wiley's yard, but they're technically not stepping foot on it. Grass is a pretty rare thing in our neighborhood. Well, in all of Rio Erizo, really. So I get why they're so enamored with it, and I can't help but smile at how clever and sneaky my little sister is. At one point, Dr. Wiley's tire swing was our second-favorite activity after the tree house, until the day it wasn't. The day he "turned on us," as Mom says.

The tire sways and swings around its tree in the post-rain breeze just as the sun peeks out from behind a cloud. It creates shadows that remind me of the eerie shapes from the pink elephant scene in *Dumbo*. I squint up at the sky and decide that it's time to head back home before Noora spirals too deep.

"Alright, little Sissies," I say as I try to coax them down the sidewalk. Their reluctant feet shuffle at a pace that's even slower than peanut butter. We barely make it a few yards before a sound forces my stomach to drop. Dr. Wiley's front door flings open with a loud bang.

"Look!" His voice booms across the grassy yard as I turn to face the house. Dr. Wiley stands on his stoop, pointing a finger toward the shadow below the tire swing. My mind is telling me to grab the littles' hands and run as fast as we can in the opposite direction, but a feeling of curiosity seeps into my brain and makes me look at the ground where he's pointing. Just to see what the big deal is about. It's so creepy, I have to look away almost immediately. The tire isn't moving anymore, and the shadow looks just like a person hanging with a rope around their neck. I can make out both feet hanging there and even their tongue hanging out of their mouth.

I grab the littles' hands before they have a chance to look at the scary hanging shadow and take off for our house. Our run isn't nearly as fast as mine would be alone, but I can't leave them. Not there, and not with Dr. Wiley. Through Lulu and Marie's grunts and grumbles, I can make out Dr. Wiley's voice.

"Witches!" he yells. He could be yelling at the swing or just into space, but I think he might be yelling at us.

CHAPTER 10

(NOW)

I SHAKE MY head back and forth, trying to dislodge the eerie image of the tire swing shadow from my mind. It tends to pop in during moments of quiet and calm, along with other disturbing images that I'd prefer to never think about. This is one reason I like to keep my mind busy — as a form of distraction.

I sometimes turn to videos of others solving mathematical problems to calm my mind. My favorite mathlete is @ FibonnaciFran, who solves follower-submitted equations on Instagram Live every Tuesday evening at 6 pm. I've submitted at least a dozen problems, but I haven't stumped her yet. She plays classical music in the background, which isn't my favorite, but I get that some people have certain tunes that help them focus. And I'll tolerate it if it means watching Fran work her magic in real time.

But the behind-the-scenes of the Live is something I'd never really considered and certainly didn't think I'd see first-hand. Yet here's Lulu, or Lumaara, rather, smack dab in my living room streaming Live. She has her tripod set up along with a backdrop on a fancy stand. The crystals hanging behind her aren't even real! They're just images printed on thick vinyl. Instead of her infamous mirrored pillows, she has a crocheted throw complete with tassel fringe.

I have a much better view of her than I did earlier, now that I've moved to the kitchen. It's nearly 11 am, which means it's almost time for lunch and well within the time window to transition from the office to the kitchen. Because I have a cut-out wall overlooking the living room, I can cook while keeping an eye on her. I grab my colander of veggies and walk over to the right side of my kitchen island, but I can't quite see her anymore. Left side, maybe? No, that doesn't feel right at all. But on the right I can't see. *Effity eff.* I walk around and around the island until I finally stop right in front of the cutout.

The way Lulu stares directly into the camera of her phone and speaks, or rather, performs for her followers is uncanny. It's like she's become an entirely different person. Something deep inside me aches. I wish I could turn into another person sometimes. Or all the time.

"Grand rising, beautiful light beings," she says. I've only seen a handful of her videos but I already know that's how she begins them all. Her voice has adopted that breathy quality again, and I try to place my finger on what it reminds me of, but I can't figure it out. A slide whistle that's run out of air? A broken bagpipe? I place the veggies down and pull my notebook out of my back pocket, then jot a note down to help transfer the thought from my head to the paper — essentially removing the worry and unsettled feeling that comes along with it in order to deal with it at a designated time later this evening. A technique I'd read about and tried to incorporate to provide me with a bit of relief. I won't know if it's working until I've collected at least a few more months of data.

"You'll never believe where I am today, my magical friends." Suddenly a ring of light floods my vision. "I'm here with my sister, Aisha!" Lulu thrusts her tripod up towards my face and I squint at the phone. Dozens of hearts and messages flood the screen as I try to push the bright circle out of my face.

"Can't you see the resemblance?" she asks, then moves her head into the frame until we're cheek to cheek.

"Lulu!" I groan, bringing my hand up to my face in an attempt to shield my eyes. My sister's expression turns ice cold as soon as the name escapes my lips. She shoots me a glare, then turns her attention back to her followers.

"Just a cute little nickname my Sissy here gave me." Lulu giggles and her nose turns pink. "But enough about my family," she adds quickly. "Let's get to the topic of today's Live. The Ace of Wands."

My heart rate slows as soon as I hear the name of the card she's discussing today. It's bad enough that she showed my face and said my full first name on social media, two things I absolutely don't do. But if she'd talked about The Hanged Man card, it would absolutely let whoever sent me the card know that I've told others. That is, if they follow Lumaara.

Lulu is seated again and performing for the camera while I mindlessly chop cucumbers for our salad. Wait, what if Dr. Wiley or whoever this mystery person is sent it to me as a way to get to her? She *is* Instagram famous, after all. So many questions, and only ones that can be answered when we figure out who sent this card.

After she says goodbye to her fans, Lulu slides into the

barstool next to where I'm hovering over the kitchen counter. I'm too anxious to eat, but as soon as I push Lulu's salad across the countertop, she grabs a fork and digs right in.

"Just over 13K," she says between bites. A small piece of carrot falls out of her mouth onto her lap and she picks it up, pops it back in, and keeps chomping away. My stomach does a flip as I try not to think about how many germs are residing on her woven skirt. I wipe down all my surfaces at least six times a day, and it's not recommended to eat food off of surfaces that haven't been sanitized properly. *Six. Six sixes are thirty-six. One thousand, two hundred and ninety-six.*

I shake my head and tilt my head to the side as I feign shoving a kalamata olive into my mouth.

Lulu recognizes that I'm completely lost and clarifies for me. "That's how many viewers I had on my Live today."

My jaw drops and the olive falls right out onto the counter.

"Holy crap," I exhale as I grab it, then drop it into the trash. Like a normal person should.

"Eh, it's not my best, but the sponsors will be happy." She shrugs and continues speaking before I can even ask about her sponsors.

"But what's really interesting is that I did a quick search on Dr. Wiley and it looks like he's still in that same creepy house." Lulu raises an eyebrow and shoots me a mischievous smirk. I can't believe he's still kicking after all this time. It felt like he was nearly a million years old when we were kids. For many years I kept tabs on old Dr. Wiley, but I suppose I assumed he'd be gone by now.

"You sure?" I ask, narrowing my eyes at her.

"One hundred percent." Lulu says matter-of-factly. "He stopped practicing soon after..." Her voice trails off as she stares down at her food, as if the words she's searching for are written on her lettuce. Finally, she adds, "Well, you know."

"Dr. Wiley wanted us dead as children, I wouldn't be surprised if he still does. Let's head over there after we eat." Lulu turns back to her salad as if going to Dr. Wiley's is a given, and if I were anyone else, it probably would be. Completely normal. But this errand is anything but normal to me. I haven't stepped foot out my front door in years.

When she arrived, I thought maybe Lu suspected that was the case, but it's becoming more and more clear that she has no idea. Or maybe she's testing me. Whatever the case, I'm grounded in my environment and have no intention of leaving this house. I just can't. No matter what.

The words are on the tip of my tongue. I wish I could tell my sister. Sure, I open the front door to retrieve my grocery delivery or leave my garbage on the stoop on Sunday evenings for the neighborhood kid I hired to drop in the trash bin, but I haven't stepped foot outside my front door in — no, I can't even think about it. It's utterly embarrassing. Even saying it in my head feels completely ridiculous. How does one become confined to their home like this?

My eyes and fists squeeze shut as I think back to 2017. It started out as a joke between myself and my remote colleagues — "Haha, A. Wren hasn't left the house in three months!" "Nine months without stepping outside? She's still going strong." "One year streak, A!" — but it quickly grew into something bigger. And possibly dangerous.

I don't even want to think about the last time I tried to step outside. A thick sense of dread settled over me and pressed down on my chest until I could barely breathe. My fingers clawed at my throat until everything turned black. Because I'd isolated myself from friends, family, neighbors, and practically everyone else in my life, no one discovered me. I finally came to on my back steps a while later and haven't ventured out since.

"I'm not feeling great, so maybe you should go alone," I say, adding a little bit of gravel to my voice to make me sound ill. It's always been my go-to excuse for not leaving. No one wants someone with the flu at their party or event. The pandemic was awful for so many reasons, but it was a blessing for agoraphobic folks like me. At least, I believed so at the time.

My sister looks up at me and narrows her eyes. "Seems like you've been fine all morning."

"Yeah, well, it came on suddenly." I shrug.

"I really need you to come with me though, Aisha."

"I *really* can't."

I abandon my salad and my feet draw me into the never-ending loop from the kitchen into the living room and back. Lulu follows me with her eyes but doesn't say anything. The uncomfortable silence makes my heart rate rise. Why isn't she saying anything? Should I say something?

"No worries, Sissy," she finally says, her voice dripping with cheer. "You can stay in the car while I see if he's home."

No. No no no no. I can't. I stop mid-pacing and get the strong urge to stomp my feet. I don't, because that would just be childish, but I can sense my inner child rising to the surface and wanting to take control. I feel like I'm about to burst.

"Lulu, you don't understand." My voice is just below a yell, and I feel my temperature rise as my underarms become moist. "I literally cannot leave this house."

She doesn't respond so I say it again, although this time it comes out as a mere whisper. "I literally can't."

Lulu's brow furrows, creasing her poreless forehead as she processes my words. A few excruciating moments pass before a flash of understanding pushes the confusion from her face. For a brief moment, my heart softens. *My sister gets it.* I have nothing to be ashamed of because there's finally someone on my side. I feel my shoulders relax and I allow my eyelids to close in deep relief, yet they snap right back open as soon as Lulu says the thing I dread the most.

"That's ridiculous, Ishie."

She dismisses me with a dramatic wave of her fork as if brushing aside my seemingly silly notion. "Of course you can leave." She goes back to eating her salad then adds, "What happened to that strong little girl with the woman's intuition?"

My little sister's words hit me like a punch to the gut. What was I thinking? I should have known better than to confide in her. How could she possibly understand? My sister and I are worlds apart. Yet I didn't expect her to have the audacity to belittle my struggles.

My temperature rises as the shame takes the shape of white hot rage. Nineteen hours I've wasted changing my whole lifestyle for this person who doesn't even care to know me. *Nineteen by nineteen is three hundred and sixty-one.* I swing the front door open and motion toward my portal.

"I think maybe you should go." I stare at Lulu and attempt to analyze her expression. Is she preparing to protest or is she getting ready to leave? I can't tell. Either way, she looks spooked.

"Well?" I say, letting my younger self shine through for a brief moment. "What's it going to be?"

"Aisha," is all she says. Her voice is breathy again.

"What?" I prod again.

"Look."

I follow her gaze to the mat in front of my door. There is a red envelope resting on it.

CHAPTER 11

(THEN)

I SLAM THE front door behind us, then slide all the way down to my butt and join Marie and Lulu on the floor in the hallway. We're all panting and soaking wet. "Why did he say… that?" Marie whispers once she catches her breath. As I peel off my wet t-shirt, I just shake my head.

"I always thought he liked us," Lulu squeaks. Her little shoulders hunch over and I can see the hurt in her eyes as I reach down to help yank off her wet shoes. With all the water in them it's like they're suction-cupped to her feet, making a big *schlurp* noise when we finally get them off. We all give a little chuckle, even though the cold is starting to set in.

"Maybe because of the spell book?" Lulu says with a sigh after we finally get the second shoe off. My head whips around so fast at the mention of our special book that my hair sends water flying across the hallway wall.

"The spell book!"

I pat down my legs and belly thinking maybe I'd forgotten I'd tucked it somewhere while looking for the littles, but it's no use. There's no way I could have held onto it throughout that adventure, and definitely no way it could be hiding in my bike shorts and Spice Girls t-shirt.

"Neither of you have it?" I ask the littles, but they simply shake their heads. "Fudgesicle!" I curse under my breath, twisting the dripping curls at the nape of my neck. I mentally try to retrace our steps. When did I last see the spell book? Probably the tree house? But that feels like so long ago. The rainwater I've wrung out of my hair is cold as it drips down my shoulders into my training bra.

"I'm freezing." Marie's lips are now a purplish color and she's shivering. Right, first things first, I need to do the big sissy thing and get Lu and Marie dried off. The book can wait.

I help the littles out of their clothes in the doorway so they don't track water around the house and get Mom all mad like last time, then wrap them up in towels before they run off to Lulu's room to change. I can totally do this big sister thing. But once we're warm and settled on the family room sofa, my mind goes back to the spell book. I'm so upset that none of us have it, so I'm really hoping that Noora or Kayla held onto it. It was really expensive! We'll have to save up again for another one. But more than anything, it was our special book. Something that connected the five of us even more than being blood sisters could. I know tons of girls my age who aren't close to their siblings and it just seems so strange to me.

As I glance over at Lulu and Marie cuddled up in the fuzzy blankets we reserve for movie nights and feel the warm fuzzies crawl over my skin, another thought pops into my brain. What if someone else finds it? Will they think we're witches just like Dr. Wiley? I can't even remember who had it last, but if it was me, the rest of the sissies will be super mad at me. I need to find it.

Both of the littles have their eyes glued to *Bambi* on the television screen, and I can't help but reach over to give Lulu's head a pat. With Noora done with high school, it'll be up to me to watch over Lu soon. I need to use the rest of the summer to practice my big sistering before Noora leaves for college. But the good news is that I'll have Kayla by my side to help me protect the littles. Lulu flattens the damp curls that I mussed up, then turns to face me.

"Ishie, do you think she got lost?" Her big eyes well up with tears and her bottom lip starts to shake. I can see her body becoming restless under the blanket — knees bouncing, feet kicking — and I hate it when that happens. That's when I know she's really upset. That, or just hungry or tired or all of the above, which is the worst combination.

"Who? Noora?" My shoulders slouch a bit at the mention of my big sister. I get that Lu is attached to her and looks up to her, but I'm big sis material, too. "No way, she's seventeen, she's fine. She'll get here soon, probably before Mom, even."

But as I say the words, I'm not sure if I believe them. Noora doesn't mess around, but she also doesn't back down when she has a problem to solve. She would probably stay out all night looking for Lulu if she had to. I start to get a little sweaty as I think about it and get up off the couch, but it'll be fine. At least I think so.

"Listen," I call to Lulu from the kitchen as I open a Tupperware of leftover deviled eggs. "If she isn't back before Mom, we'll have Mom drive us toward the tree house to pick Noora and Kayla up, OK?" Lu nods her head and takes the bowl of deviled eggs, tiny carrots, and baby corn from me, then digs in. I knew she was probably starving. Another big sister win for me!

As Lulu and Marie munch away on their afternoon snack, the sound of the car pulling into the driveway pulls them both toward the front window.

"Mommy!" Lulu announces.

I head to the window with them, but instead of feeling relieved, I feel a little uneasy. I was sure Noora and Kayla would be here by now because the trail down to the tree house and the part of the arroyo where we hang out really isn't that big. It shouldn't take them that long to search, then realize the littles are home with me. Unless they think Lulu and Marie roamed outside of our usual spots. My stomach does a flip. They could really be anywhere by now.

I head to the front door and fling it open, but I don't run out with the other girls. I shift from side to side and squeeze my hands at my hips as I try to predict how Mom will react. Will she be mad that I separated from Noora and Kayla? Will she be relieved that I found the littles? Did I wipe up the dribbles of water on the entryway well enough? What about the spell book? I don't have much time to think because the van door opens right then and Mom steps out.

The look on her face is way too hard to read. Luckily, the side door slides open right after and out pop Noora and Kayla. My heart unsticks itself from my throat and moves back down to its usual place, in my chest. Is this how Noora feels all the time? Maybe this big sister thing is harder than I thought.

CHAPTER 12

(NOW)

Two cards. Two cryptic tarot cards delivered to my front door. *Two twos are four, four fours are sixteen.*

I didn't think things could get any creepier, but this message makes me physically ill. I'm inching closer and closer to the edge, desperately hoping that a big gust of wind doesn't knock me into a darkness I cannot come back from. Just as before, the blood red envelope contains a tarot card. It's worn, with edges that are frayed and stained. I can make out a faint ring on the back of the card through the delicate mandala pattern. It's dark red, like the ring from a wine glass. At least I hope it's wine.

Instead of an image of someone hanging upside down, it shows a hooded figure holding a staff in one hand and a lantern in the other.

"The Hermit," Lulu breathes from over my shoulder. "What does it say?"

My sister's long feather earrings tickle my ears as she moves from shoulder to shoulder, trying to get a closer peek at the tarot card. My insides clench when I feel her hot breath on my neck. I haven't been this close to anyone in who knows how long.

I'd toyed with not opening this envelope, just as I'd done with the first. But of course, the not knowing was far too strong. It sunk its claws into me and wouldn't release its grasp until I'd torn into the envelope. Lulu just stared at me with her head tilted to the side and an eyebrow raised as I let the envelope flutter to the ground, then collapsed into the couch.

"Here," I muster, shoving it into her hands. I can't look at it any longer.

"When solitude's grip tightens, ensnaring like thorns, madness envelops the unsuspecting hermit. Beware the fated descent." She reads the message scribbled along the border of the card aloud while squinting to make out the small letters. I can hear her hard swallow as she traces the chilling image with her pointer finger.

"…unsuspecting hermit…fated descent?" Lulu rereads the words several times at a whisper, and brings the card closer to her face as her voice gets quieter. As she analyzes the message, one element of the card keeps sticking out to me. My mathematical brain goes to work and I can't hold back from sharing my findings with my sister.

"It says IX at the top," I say. "And nine is actually a really special number." I pause and wait for a response but am greeted with more silence. "If I had to pick a favorite number, it would probably be nine. Not only is it a perfect square, but if you multiply nine by any number, then add the digits together until you get a single digit, it always comes out to nine." I guess not everyone loves mathematics as much as I do. I resist telling her more about the magic of nine and instead eagerly wait for her to tell me what she's thinking. But her scrunched eyebrows tell me that she's deep in thought.

After what feels like hours but is really only a few long minutes, I break the heavy silence. "So, what do you think?"

Lulu rubs her temples, her stacks of bangles clanking together with the gesture. I notice new webs of red creeping across the whites of her eyes that weren't there earlier. Perhaps this is weighing on her as much as it is me.

"I mean, isn't it obvious?" she finally says.

I furiously shake my head no, because it's definitely not obvious to me.

"Aisha, you're The Hermit."

Lulu's words hang heavy in the room. I can't even begin to deny that she's speaking the truth. She knows that I can't leave, but I don't think she has a clue about the full extent of my isolation. However, it's not Lulu's opinion of me that's sending chills down my spine. It's the notion that someone else knows. That someone's been watching me.

When I finally gaze up at Lulu, she's studying me intently. The judgment I thought I'd seen in her eyes not even half an hour ago has softened into something resembling empathy. And maybe a little pity.

"How long has it been?"

My jaw clenches at the question. I don't know if I have the strength to answer truthfully, but I certainly don't have the energy to fabricate an answer or offer my usual excuses. I don't even look up to meet her eyes before I say the words.

"Seven years."

The weight of the truth crashes into me like a wave breaking and I gasp from the impact. It's been nearly a decade since

I left these walls. So much has happened on the outside world since then, and I missed it all.

I look to my sister and Lulu's already-big eyes grow even more. I cover my own face with my hands. *Seven sevens are forty-nine, forty-nine by forty-nine is two thousand, four hundred and one.* Why did I tell her? Why didn't I say seven months? Or seven weeks?

"No, no, don't do that," she says, delicately placing her hand on my knee. This time, I don't pull away. Lulu uses her long nails to gently trace little swirls and what feel like symbols on my leg. My breathing slows and deepens, and I notice my heart rate drop back to its usual rhythm.

"The hermit isn't alone for selfish or shameful reasons, Ishie." Her voice mimics the tender gestures. "Taking a sec to look within is a form of self-care, but like with anything, too much of anything can be a bad thing. That's probably what the 'madness envelopes the unsuspecting hermit' means in the message."

"Whenever I pull The Hermit card for someone," she continues, "it's usually a reminder that they need to find a balance between isolation and interaction. And do you see how he's holding a lantern?" Lulu points to the tarot card now resting on my coffee table and I silently nod. "A lot of people refer to it as the Lamp of Truth, and I like to view it as an invitation to let your inner truth guide you. Light the way, you know?"

I look up but can't seem to meet her gaze. Everything Lulu says is right, but it doesn't feel like it's applicable to me. I'm simply not like most of the people for whom she reads tarot cards. Because of my sticky brain and deeply-rooted fears, isolating myself has become the only option. Not to mention, my inner truth and anxiety have intermingled for so long, it's practically impossible for me to discern one from the other.

"What's going on in that brain of yours?" Lulu stops tickling my knee and instead just stares at me intently with one eyebrow cocked. A sputtery laugh escapes my lips that it's that obvious my mind is spinning, but also because I have absolutely no way of expressing what's going on up there. It's way too complex — I wouldn't even know where to start.

"It's just way easier said than done," I shrug weakly. My thoughts flash back to the stacks of self-help books I've read, the "transformational" courses I've completed, the hours of talk therapy, and the gaping hole these techniques have failed to fill. If I had a Lamp of Truth, I would have found it by now. Instead, the hollowness in my core continues growing. I purse my lips and rub the back of my neck.

"Well, yeah. I mean, everything takes work, Ishie."

If only she knew the amount of work I *have* put in.

"I just think I need serious work. Not just 'a little push' of motivation, but professional help or something…" My voice trails off as my eyes find the floor again, then I whisper a question that I've been too afraid to utter to anyone.

"What if I've already descended into madness?" I look down at my hands.

Silence seeps across the space between us, but instead of being an unsettling silence that I feel forced to fill, it's a comforting silence. A knowing silence. Though Lulu finally breaks it with something that makes me anxious.

"Do you ever think about Noora?"

My body instinctively pulls backwards and my muscles go rigid at the mention of her name. I shouldn't be surprised that Lulu brought her up. She was such a huge part of our lives. Even though Lulu and I were close before the accident, Noora was always the glue that kept us together. Her departure from our lives was a huge loss for both of us. Though we clearly grieved in very different ways.

"Of course." The words come out as a mere squeak. "Do you?"

"Yeah, all the time. You just haven't mentioned her at all since I got here and I'm a little surprised, is all," Lulu says. Her eyes are on her nails as she works to push her cuticles back.

"Well, there's not much to say." I shrug.

Lulu's hand finds my knee again and gives it a tight squeeze. "She was such a big part of our childhoods. I mean, she kind of shaped who we are. And even though she's not a part of your life anymore, she can still help you."

We lock eyes and a momentary pulse of energy seems to flow between us. But my gaze is pulled away by a movement in the window. My heart leaps in anticipation for my hummingbirds who seem to know exactly when I need them. Watching their little wings move as a harmonious blur always helps bring my anxiety down and ground me, and I need that type of therapy right now more than anything. But when I turn toward the window to greet my hummers, they're not there.

Instead, I see a man staring back at me.

CHAPTER 13

(NOW)

My heart races as I struggle to scream, but I'm frozen. My mouth won't open, and even if it could, I'm not sure any noise would escape. I lock eyes with the person standing in my back-yard for just a moment and he looks about as surprised to see me as I am him. He's so close, practically a foot away from where I'm sitting on the couch. Just a pane of glass between us. Twelve inches away. *Twelve twelves are one hundred and forty-four.* I can make out the gold flecks in his deep brown eyes and wispy pieces of sandy brown hair peeking out from under a blood red beanie. The air around me feels like it's closing in, pressing on my lungs and forcing me in place.

If only I could lift my arms, I would leap forward and bang on the window and confront him. Demand to know why he's there, what he wants, and whether he's connected to the mysterious tarot cards. Meanwhile, the part of me that isn't paralyzed by fear works to make sense of this. For all I know he got lost coming up from the arroyo or is taking a shortcut to get down there, but I'm me, so, of course, my mind instinctively reaches for the worst case scenario: he's here to hurt me. Or my sister.

"Ishie? You good?" Lulu tilts her head to look in the direction I'm staring, but he's already ducked out of sight. Her gaze turns back to me and her perfectly threaded eyebrows are now knotted with concern.

"You're lookin' a little green," she says. Lulu's hands find mine and give them a reassuring squeeze. "I think maybe all this talk of Noora is a little too much for today."

But as she slowly rises off the couch, my heart rate continues to skyrocket. "Th-there's someone," I finally sputter, "someone in my yard."

"What?" Lulu breathes. "Are you sure?" She rushes toward the back door, her hair waving and flowy skirt dancing behind as she jogs to the other side of the house.

I finally force my legs to move and follow. I hadn't realized just how petite my younger sister is until I notice her rise up on her bare tippy toes to peek out the doorlight.

"Where?" she demands as she presses her face up against the glass pane. Her cheeks are flushed, and I'm slightly comforted to know that she appears as panicked as I am. I point a shaking hand toward the left side of the house where I saw him duck, then describe what he is wearing along with the horrified look on his face.

Lulu flings the door open and steps out into the brisk late afternoon air. I take a step toward the door frame, feeling the rays of sun kiss my skin. In the distance, the azure sky is peppered with fluffy clouds. Even though I'm just inches away from the outside world, I'm surprisingly calm. My feet are still planted safely within my house and my sister is nearby. But not for long. In the blink of an eye, she leaps down the steps and around the corner, out of sight.

"Are you seriously still in the same spot?" Lulu bursts through the juniper bushes on the other side of the yard, sending me off balance. I reach out and steady myself with the cold door frame, careful not to fall forward down the steps.

"Well, you were only gone for a few minutes," I reply, eagerly wringing my hands and waiting for an update on the lurker.

"Try forty-five," she says with a raised eyebrow.

I close my eyes and breathe in the herbaceous scent of the juniper bordering my yard.

"Oh, wow." I hadn't realized it had been that long — the pulse of the humming cicadas must have lulled me into a meditative state. They sound like a symphony against the setting sun. It's not hard to become intoxicated by the fresh air and whimsy of the New Mexico landscape. They don't call this state the "Land of Entrapment" for nothing.

"Did you find him, though?" The words fly out of my mouth and are greeted by a deliberate head shake.

"Nope, I ran all over your block but didn't see any guys in beanies," she reports. As she speaks, Lulu's feet stop directly in front of mine. She's so close to me, I can smell the peppermint gum on her breath.

"Look, Ish, I love you, no matter what's happened between us, but it's really hard for me to see you like this." She motions toward the ground: my feet firmly planted on my kitchen tile, and hers on the dusty concrete step. I feel my heart clench. But instead of feeling like an embarrassment, the warmth of what she said covers me like a soft blanket.

"Which is why I'm making you a pot of Maaji's ginger chai to help feed your soul and soothe your nerves." Lulu gently grabs hold of my shoulders and spins my body around, then guides me toward the living room.

"That does sound really good…" I smile, letting myself fall onto the couch.

We curl up on either end of the sofa, sharing a blanket just like we used to when we were kids. The combination of the warm tea in my belly and the melodic dance of the humming-birds at my window, with the stunning New Mexico sunset as a backdrop, makes me almost forget about the creepy tarot cards. The stranger by my window. My sister's reemergence in my life. I'm almost feeling safe and secure enough that, even though I count the number of birds buzzing through my field of vision — there are eight unique birds that I've identified, including Blaze — I allow my eyes to focus on the rom-com movie Lulu chose and my mind to quiet before I even have a chance to multiply eight by eight.

Is this what it feels like? To not be tortured by the need to count or control every moment of my life? To let go of the never-ending loop of anxiety and compulsions that I've found myself trapped in? For the first time in a long time, I feel a sense of peace envelop me. I welcome the tear that rolls down my cheek as my eyelids become heavy.

Just a few minutes to rest my eyes. Then we'll get back to work.

CHAPTER 14

(THEN)

IF ONLY KEEPING tears in was as easy as squeezing your eyes shut, kinda like how you can hold your pee in by squeezing your legs together. I'm just so relieved to see Noora and Kayla that a few tears end up escaping from my eyes. But I wipe them away before anyone can see.

Stress isn't a feeling I know very well. Love, yeah, especially when I see a cute cat or dog. Joy, totally. Anger, sometimes — mostly when I'm dealing with my sisters. I just don't really worry. Mom says Noora inherited all of her anxiety, and she didn't have any left when she made me. Instead, I'm her "gutsy girl" who doesn't think twice before taking action.

But the idea of having to tell Mom that I have no idea where Noora and Kayla are did kind of cause a big pit to form in my belly. So when I see them hop out of the mini-van, I can feel it morph into happiness almost immediately. My big sister is gritting her teeth, though, and I can see that big vein in her forehead starting to pop out. *Uh oh.*

"What the heck, Aisha?" Noora grabs onto the edge of my t-shirt and drags me into her bedroom, then shuts the door.

"Well, I found them, didn't I?" I don't want to look right into her eyes, so instead I look at all the posters across her wall. Britney, Shakira, Aaliyah, and Christina — all the girls are here.

"That's not the point." If they had an eye-rolling championship, Noora would win every single time. I had no idea someone's eyes could even go back that far. "You just disappeared! You could have been hurt!" she says almost in a whisper-shout. "Don't ever do that again."

"You can't tell me what to do." I cross my arms as my words jab back at her. When we get like this, I can't help thinking about the jousters at the Renaissance Faire. They race toward each other with a pointy lance, whereas we poke at each other with our words. I'm making sure mine are extra sharp because I'm not about to fall off my horse right now. "You're not Mom."

At that, Noora gets right up in my face. "No, I'm not, but there's no way I'm going to tell Mom what happened because I don't want her to find out we lost the littles." She's so close I can smell the egg on her breath that Lulu gave her because she was so worried Noora had gotten too hungry out there.

Even if she is being kinda dramatic and scary, Noora makes a good point. If Mom found out we'd been separated, she'd definitely freak out. I nod and mumble a defeated "fine" before leaning back against her closed door.

"Aisha, I'm counting on you." Noora's face softens as she says it, and I can finally see my caring big sister again through that angsty teenage exterior.

I let my head fall and stare at my big toe sticking out the end of my ripped sock. It's just hanging out there with nothing to protect it. Just like Lulu. She'll be without protection when Noora leaves if I don't get my stuff together and start acting like the big sister I know I can be. I wiggle my toe back into my sock, then bend down to tie a few of the stray sock strands together.

"Ish?" Noora's voice isn't soft anymore. "Are you even listening to me?" I can see out the corner of my eye that she's waving her hand in front of me, like an "Earth to Aisha!" kinda gesture, but my mind is somewhere else. First on my sock, and now on Lulu.

I snap upright and wiggle my toe, but it stays snug and safe inside the sock. I did it! Better yet, I have an idea of how I can protect Lu: a protection spell from the book! It'll help for a little bit at least, like those sock strings, until I can be the big sister she deserves.

"Yeah, I got it!" I say in Noora's direction, but I'm already out her bedroom door and racing down the hall to find my bestie. She's on the couch, tossing popcorn up into the air and catching it in her mouth.

"Hey," I shout, digging my hand into the bowl of popcorn on her lap. "When do you two need to be home?" Kayla flinches from surprise, but her eyes quickly light up and a smile forms across her face when she jokingly pulls the bowl away.

"We don't! Our mom said we can sleep over if it's OK with your mom."

"Perfect!" I grab the bowl from her and set it on the coffee table, then grab her hands and hoist her off the couch. "We need to find the spell book. I have an idea."

"Oh yeah?" A sneaky smile forms on Kayla's lips.

Noora shouts from her room. "The sun sets at 8:15, so make sure you're back on the street by eight."

"OK!" Kayla and I shout back in unison. As we skip out the door and back onto Cactus Creek, I feel the warm breeze lift the damp flyaway hairs off my neck — and feel someone's eyes on the back of my head.

CHAPTER 15

(NOW)

HOW LONG HAS it been? I jolt upright and blink my eyes open, but the room is pitch black. How on Earth did I fall asleep on my couch? Although it's not really that surprising considering I barely got any sleep last night before Lulu's arrival, and the entire day has been a roller coaster of emotions. A perfect storm for an extended nap.

One of the reasons I hate napping is because the wakeup is so jarring. Particularly if you fall asleep during dusk, then wake up after the sun has set. Like I just did.

A quick glance at my watch indicates that it's not even night anymore, but the wee hours of the morning — 3:33 am, to be exact. Lulu would probably get a kick out of that, knowing how spiritual and woo she is now. *Three threes are nine, nine by nine is eighty-one. Six thousand, five hundred and sixty-one.*

Anxiety twists in my belly as I realize that time is slipping away. Precious hours are gone that we could have used to find the answers I so desperately seek. We can't afford to let our guard down again.

I groan as I rise to my feet. "Oh god, I can't believe this." My hand tenderly presses into the right side of my neck, though I wince as soon as I make contact. Erratic sleeping positions are not kind to an aging body; Ibuprofen is definitely in order. I motion to turn on the light but quickly remember that it's not just me here. My sister's staying over, even though the far end of the couch is now empty. She must have dragged herself to bed, something I wish I'd had the foresight to do.

It occurs to me that it might not just be the two of us here. I trudge to the window, my heart pounding with every step. After several minutes of silent observation, I reason that there's no one lurking outside. I even open the back door and peek into the backyard, but it's just me and the darkness.

On tip-toe, I make my way into the kitchen to avoid waking Lulu and evaluate the state of my house. I have time scheduled into my evening routine to tidy up the house so as to not wake up to a mess, but clearly Lulu doesn't have the same objective. I shouldn't be surprised. My masala dabba — a traditional Indian spice box that holds all my cooking and chai spices — was left open all night and my nose is assaulted by the pungent aroma of garam masala as soon as I walk into the kitchen. Cold tea is still sitting in the glass kettle on the stove, and the counter is covered with splashes of the milky concoction and dirty dishes.

I do my best to clean up the mess while staying as silent as possible, but I make a wrong move and send a handful of spoons flying into the sink, creating a deafening clatter. *Effity eff eff.*

My body remains motionless and I hold my breath for several seconds, listening to hear if Lulu stirs, but I don't hear a peep. I think I'm in the clear, but I still tiptoe toward my second bedroom — I can't really call it a guest room, since I never truly have guests, at least, not until this weekend — and peek inside the open door to confirm I didn't wake her.

But instead of finding my sister sleeping soundly on the sleeper sofa, the room is empty. Her bag is lackadaisically tossed on the floor but still zipped up. It doesn't look like she ever got ready for bed. I wander around the house switching on every light I come across, hoping I'll find her curled up on my reading chair or in my own bed — but my house is completely empty.

I grab my phone off the coffee table and, after locating the number she'd DM'd me on Instagram, begin dialing. Each unanswered call feels like an eternity. I leave voicemails and send urgent text messages. "Call me as soon as you get this. Please tell me you're safe. I'm freaking out right now." I pace around the house, the outgoing calls, messages, and panic continuing until the sun begins to peek over the Sangre de Cristo Mountains and stream in from my east-facing windows.

I finally have my sister back in my life and now I've lost her just as quickly. I can't let that happen. My silent prayers are finally answered when I see her name pop up on my phone. I swallow the wave of emotions surging through me and try to steady my voice as I answer the call.

CHAPTER 16

(NOW)

"LULU, WHAT THE eff?" I jump off the couch and stand in the center of my living room as I scream into the phone. All I can hear on the other end is hysterical laughing.

"Hello? Lu?" The panic oozes off my words, but I'm still only greeted with eerie chuckles.

"It's a FaceTime, you dork!" My sister's words come through loud and clear, and on speaker. I pull the phone away from my ear when I realize my blunder and start pacing through the kitchen and living room. The counters are pristine and glistening after my panic-cleaning session while I waited for her call. Or waited until daylight so I could call the police. Whichever came first.

"It's not funny," I growl, though I'm incredibly relieved to not only hear my sister's voice but also see her modelesque face beaming back at me. I gather that she's outdoors, based on the subtle sound of the wind whistling through the phone and the trees swaying in the background. Lulu's flawless complexion radiates like bronze as the morning sun shines down on her. My sister truly is a goddess. No wonder so many people worship her on social media.

In my head I'd reasoned that she'd either been abducted by the man who appeared in my window or the tarot card stalker — maybe they were one and the same. Perhaps a frenzied fan decided to track her down and snatch her up? *What if I'd harmed her myself?* Then cleaned up the evidence and disposed of her body without any recollection. I'd come across an article last year about a woman who found herself in a similar position where she'd sleep-walked and murdered her entire family — people she cared for deeply — while in a delusional dream-like state. My thoughts had transformed from, *How does someone do that?* to *What if I'm capable of doing that?* and, in that moment, a new fear was unlocked. The fear had stayed dormant for so long, but it quickly made its way to the surface and reared its ugly head when I faced the reality of a missing loved one of my own. Whatever the case, there was no plausible explanation for my sister's sudden disappearance. She wouldn't just leave, or would she?

"Where did you go? I was so worried," I demand.

"I thought you always said worrying was Mom's job, not Noora's, and definitely not yours." Lulu's demeanor is as cheerful as ever.

"Yeah, well neither of them are here right now, are they?" I snap back. For a moment all I can see are the whites of her eyes as my sister rolls her eyes at my retort. Her thick waves bounce and dance behind her as she walks against the wind.

A trail of sidewalk spans behind her and, as the adobe homes come into view, I have a sense that they look eerily familiar.

"What time did you leave my house? Why did you just leave? And where have you been?" The questions pour out of me. "Where are you anyway, Lu?" I ask, but as soon as the words escape my lips, I see the lush green lawn and the tire swing swaying in the breeze come into view beside her. The sight makes my stomach drop and I reach backward to find the couch, then settle into the cushion, allowing it to swallow my body along with my panic.

"Wait, you went to Dr. Wiley's?"

"Yeah, of course I did." Lulu shifts her eyes but it's her tone that hints she's annoyed. Likely with me. "I couldn't sleep, so I figured I'd do some exploring to make the most of our time." She gives me a sideways glance. "I told you I was going to talk to Dr. Wiley."

Lulu's right. She did say that. I just didn't think she'd go so soon. And certainly not in the middle of the night.

"And… what'd you find?" I sit upright on the very edge of the couch, my right leg jiggling with anxiety as I wait for her to give me the news. *Was he even home? Was he the sender of the red envelopes?* My heart races with anticipation, longing for closure and peace at last. No more red envelopes or eerie messages. An opportunity to move forward. A feeling of hope flutters up from my belly and gets caught in my throat as I realize this could be an opportunity for me and my sister to reconnect and stay in each other's lives. *Finally.*

"It's not him." She drops the words like a too-heavy bag and I'm taken down with them. I'm back to square one. Lulu sees my hand rise up to caress my brow as I slump back into the soft upholstery. "I'm so sorry, Ishie."

"Are you sure, though?" This time I'm really just thinking

out loud. "Did you actually talk to him? Do you think he'd actually admit it? What if he's lyi—"

"Trust me, Aisha," she interrupts, stopping abruptly in the middle of the sidewalk at the end of the block. "It's not him, but it'll be OK. We'll figure this out." She pulls the phone away from her body and motions as if she's hugging the phone with her free arm, then adds, "Together."

I can't help but smile as she begins describing the next steps in our investigation. There are apparently plenty of other divination techniques we can use in our pursuit for answers. She mentions dowsing rods, pendulums, and tea leaves, among other tools. I hold onto her every word, eager to put the past behind us and shape a future with my little sister.

But the grin slips off my face just as quickly as it appeared because, in the corner of the FaceTime frame, a person comes into view. They're walking on the sidewalk far behind Lulu, but there's no mistaking that sandy brown hair and blood red beanie.

CHAPTER 17

(THEN)

Every few steps, I whip my head around and look behind us, hoping to see someone there. I mean, I don't *want* someone to be following us, but if they're there, I'd like to catch them in the act and then tell them to get lost. But as the hot sun hits my skin, so does an unsettling thought: what if it's an adult following us and not a kid? My feet slow down as I imagine someone way bigger than both me and Kayla put together lurking in the shadows along our path. They could easily snatch us up, like our parents and teachers always warned us about. "Make sure you stay vigilant!" Mom always reminded us. "If you see a white van, run!" I look around but don't see anything obvious. But sometimes it's the least obvious threats that are actually the biggest ones.

When I told her I had a weird feeling as soon as we left the house, Kayla took it seriously. Just like I knew she would. She'd suggested we stop for a second to wait and listen, so we sat on the short adobe wall that separates the sidewalk from the front yards and stayed still for a few minutes. I strained my eyes and ears searching for something. Anything. But all we heard were the chirps of the birds coming from the big cactus in front of the Wellesley's house and a few lizards that scurried across the wall. The heat coming out of the rough surface felt good on my still-pruney fingers and made me feel a bit like my normal, worry-free self. Maybe it was just a couple of goofy kids. Or maybe it was absolutely nothing.

"Ish," Kayla said, nudging my fingers with hers. Her fingernails still had little fireworks of blue polish on them from our last girly "spa day." I wouldn't say we're really girly girls, but Kayla has definitely cared more about how she looks lately. Which probably has something to do with her wanting to do that Fluttering Heart Charm. I wondered who she has a crush on, but if she wanted me to know, I knew she'd tell me. I looked down at my bare nails. My polish wore off almost immediately after our spa day from all the digging and playing.

"Even if someone does randomly jump out of the bushes, you're ready for anything," she assured me. "You know that, right?" Her chocolate eyes looked especially like Hershey's Kisses when I finally looked away from the swaying juniper bushes in the Wellesley's yard. With her fine strawberry blonde hair and freckles, Kayla should have super blue eyes. I actually even told her once that she looked like she would be allergic to anything — sickly, kinda. That definitely made her laugh. So much so that she almost fell out of her chair in Ms. Parson's class. It was the first time I heard her snorty laugh and the moment I knew we needed to be friends. But somehow Kayla got these deep brown eyes that were so dark they practically swallowed up her pupils.

Seeing her look at me like that with her chocolaty eyes and reassuring smile and feeling her positive energy through our touching fingertips made me feel completely unstoppable. I felt my body swell up with pride, like I was about to lift off the ground and float away. Kayla believed in me, and I knew I could tackle whatever came my way because I always had. And that meant I could do the same for Lulu. Still, the protection spell felt like a good first step, just to make sure. We needed to find that spell book, and soon.

Together, we hopped off the rough wall, the stucco scratching the back of our bare thighs, but I barely even noticed — I had more important things on my mind, and a little scrape never bothered me — and started walking down the street again in search of our precious book. But the worry chased the hope away and followed us around like a hungry puppy. It got closer and closer until it finally nipped right at my heels.

"I've never seen you so paranoid, Ish!" Kayla yells at me from the far end of the sidewalk.

As we get farther and farther away from home, and closer and closer to creepy Dr. Wiley's house, I realize that I need Kayla's reminder that I'm acting too much like my older sister. *Anyone who runs into us is in for a big surprise,* I tell myself. *We've totally got this.* I give my cheeks a little slap to smack it out of me, then take off running toward Kayla, a new idea burning at the front of my brain.

"Race you!" I shout as I sprint past her, taking a sharp right turn down the cross street toward the Rio Grande. Maybe if we take a different route back toward the tree house and run super-fast, we could lose the stalker and still have some luck finding the spell book. I'm pretty sure it's near the tree house, sitting there in its protective plastic bag just waiting for us.

My steps get closer together as the ground beneath me

changes from concrete to firm dirt. I hear Kayla's snorty laugh from behind me. "Wait," she yells. "Where are we going?" But I already know she'll go along with it regardless.

"A shortcut through the river!"

CHAPTER 18

(NOW)

It's definitely him. His hair is that same light brown color —
almost like the color of driftwood, and it appears to lay like
driftwood too — random chunks twisted and sticking out at
awkward angles. I can't get a good look at his eyes, though,
because his gaze stays fixed on his phone as he ambles toward
my sister.

She appears completely oblivious, still chattering on about
dowsing rods as the man gets closer and closer to her.

Of course, I want to shout. Scream. Flail my hands around
and tell her to run as fast as she can, but it's happening again.
I'm in a frozen state and can't so much as open my mouth to
make any kind of sound to bring her attention to her environment. The panic has my vocal chords in one hand and my heart
in the other. When my mind isn't betraying me, my body does,

and in the most critical moments.

If he tries to hurt her, someone would see, right? Someone else must be around her. A couple taking their morning walk with their beloved pooch in tow or a student loading their car up with textbooks before heading off to campus? My eyes dart around the background, hoping to see another figure. At least my eyes still work.

Lulu stops speaking mid-sentence and gives me a warm look. "You OK?" She must sense my unease even through the phone screen. As little girls we used to be connected that way — maybe we still are.

"Mmmm," is all I can get out. The man is right there, on her tail. Can't she hear him approaching? My pulse quickens as he gets closer and closer until he's standing immediately behind her.

"Aisha? What's wrong?" This time, he looks up from his own phone. Against the backdrop of Dr. Wiley's yard in the distance, I can make out both gold and green flecks in his eyes. His gaze meets mine.

Run Lulu, now! I want to scream. But before I can even open my mouth to attempt a sound, I see his hand reach out over my sister's shoulder and toward the phone. Then the call cuts out.

He has her. He has my sister. I leap from the couch, staring at the phone in my hand through a veil of tears. With trembling fingers and a racing heart, I hit redial. She has to pick up. She has to. But she doesn't. I call eighty-one times and send twenty-seven texts. *Twenty-seven by twenty-seven is seven hundred and twenty-nine.*

Without a second thought I race toward the front door and fling it open.

"Lulu," I shriek at the top of my lungs, then crumple to

the ground in a heap of sobs. I feel overwhelmed with guilt at not being able to protect my sister. And now, I feel utterly powerless.

I push myself up into a seated position, wiping the salty tears from my cheeks. My knees pull in towards my chest and I wrap my arms around them. A new fear surfaces as I stare into the street: if I don't find my sister, I'll remain in this prison of my own doing. I could be alone forever.

As I peer longingly past the door frame at the outside world, I imagine what it must feel like out there. What I would feel like out there. To be free. My gaze sweeps over the xeriscaped front yard, which I haven't stepped foot on in years, along the desert rosemary and prickly pear cacti. Something red catches the corner of my eye and I expect to see Blaze dart through the swarm of hummingbird feeders to the right of my door, but it's not her.

I rub my eyes in disbelief at what I'm seeing: there's another red envelope tucked under my welcome mat.

CHAPTER 19

(NOW)

THIS FEELS VERY much like déjà vu. I'm practically back to square one, carrying the eerie red envelope to my office again. As I settle into my desk chair, I feel the "just right" thoughts tugging at me – the need to straighten the pens sitting in my cup holder, counting them as I do, and the uneven feeling of my shirt resting on my shoulders – but they're overpowered by a heavy sense of dread. Now it's not just my need for answers fueling this exploration, my sister's life is on the line.

My hummingbirds buzz in the background and I take a quick peek at them to calm my nerves. *If only you could tell me what to do next, my little hummers,* I think, then refocus my attention on this envelope. My immediate and possibly even my whole future depends on this. I carefully slide my finger under the thick cardstock and tear it open, revealing yet another tarot card. This is becoming par for the course, but my body still reacts to the scary image and message written on the front. Goosebumps spread like wildfire along my arms and extend all the way up to my ears.

This card feels so animalistic compared to the others. The image is a creature that looks to be half-man and half-goat. Horns are sprouting out of the top of his head, and the foreboding look in his eyes sends chills down my spine.

It's The Devil card.

I remember mention of this card from my initial research after receiving the first one, but there's no question about which card this is. I've always associated goats with Satan himself because every depiction of the devil I've ever seen has had creepy, sideways slitted eyes, just like a goat. That's why when everyone was going wild over apparently "adorable" baby goat videos during the pandemic, all I could see were furry little demons.

My eyes trace the handwritten message around the border of the image: "The Devil's seductive whispers lead souls to their own demise, with the thorny embrace of obsession as its guide."

What does it mean? Is this a threat? A warning? Or were the other cards meant to warn me and it's now too late? My mind races as I let my body fold in half and my torso and arms drape across my desk, resting my forehead on the cool wood. *Seductive whispers, demise, obsession, seductive whispers, demise, obsession.* The words feel stuck within the folds of my brain and repeat on a loop while images of the man who took Lulu flood my mind. His penetrating eyes haunts me even when I squeeze my eyes shut. Could he be the devil? My fist pounds down on the solid desk, over and over, until I feel something cool soaking into my sleeve. I look down to see the tarot card floating in liquid.

"No!" I shout as I snap upright and snatch the card between my fingers, saving it from my spilled cold cup of lavender tea. There's no way I can let this get destroyed — it's the only thing I have that could help me get to Lulu.

As I mop up the tea from my desk and dry the card, I can't stop thinking about my sister's smiling face on my phone screen. I'm supposed to be the big sister — her protector. And I really haven't been the best sibling to her, certainly not in the last decade. But I can make up for it now. I must. With a new sense of determination, I grab my phone and start fervently scrolling.

"Grand rising, beautiful light beings, and welcome back to my channel." Lulu's face fills my phone screen as I pace the comfortable path around my kitchen and living room. I wish I was seeing her on FaceTime again, but instead, I'm watching one of her old Instagram Reels, hoping to get a little insight into what the sender could be trying to tell me with this third card.

"The Devil card can be a little alarming at first glance, but don't worry." Lulu looks at the camera with compassion and reassurance beaming from her eyes, as if she's speaking directly to me. I imagine all of her viewers feel this way — like she's talking right to them. She's incredibly good at what she does. "This card doesn't have anything to do with Satan, monsters, or evil spirits. Instead, it speaks to any negative patterns in your life."

I stop pacing as soon as she says it. I feel a chill pass through me. I clutch the phone tighter. "That could be a habit, addiction, obsession, fear, or any other negative pattern that has been holding you back from living the life you desire. What is standing in your way, dear light being?"

Just as she did in her other videos, Lulu leans forward and brings her face closer to the camera. I can almost feel her hand on mine, preparing me for what she's about to say. "Deep down, you likely know exactly what it is, and this card is your sign to shine a light on it and address it once and for all." The previous messages were all deeply personal, but this one hits way too close to home. Yes, I do know exactly what is holding me back, but I don't know where to even begin in addressing it. How does the sender know exactly what is going on in my life? How long have they been watching me?

Lulu gives her signature wink and adds, "It'll be tough, but you are so much tougher. You can conquer it, and you will…"

The video continues playing, but my attention is yanked from my sister's face in the video to the notification at the top of my phone screen.

Lumaara333 added to their story.

Even though I should probably feel relieved, my stomach clenches and paranoia crawls over my skin. She didn't answer any of my frantic calls or texts, so why is she suddenly posting on her Instagram? My mind races for a logical explanation. Someone else must have her phone, that's the only plausible answer.

I quickly tap the notification before it has a chance to disappear. As the photo loads, I throw a hand over my mouth to hold back a scream.

CHAPTER 20

(THEN)

KAYLA'S VOICE ECHOES down the entire Rio Grande. "Echo!" she screams again, then laughs so hard the sound travels up and escapes out her nose. Normally I'd join her, but I still have a weird feeling and don't want to draw too much attention to us. What if someone followed us down here?

"Shhhhhh, keep it down, Kay." I move my outstretched hands downward like I'm trying to bring her voice down a few levels. If only it were that easy. It's so much quieter down here near the water; I can make out every single bird chirp and bug buzz, except when Kayla is yelling, of course. As we move over the roots, leaves, and uneven ground, our feet make a crunchy noise.

"Oh, right," Kayla whispers, stopping to gaze into the river. I join her, curious what has caught her eye. The earthy smell of the branches floating in and around the water hits me right in the nose as soon as I bend over.

"It's never this high," Kayla says in a hushed voice, then giggles and keeps walking. She's right. The rain must have brought the water level up because I don't think I've ever seen this much down here. A flicker of concern passes through me, but I brush it away along with the cottonwood fluffs that keep falling into my hair.

"All this water reminds me of the first spell we did!" Kayla continues as we march along the water in a single file line. There's never quite enough room on this trail for us to walk side by side without one person stepping into the vegetation along the trail or falling right into the river. "Do you remember, Ish?"

We've done so many different spells, I honestly can't even remember the first one we did. There's been the Stardust Memory Tea, Fairy Whisper Spell, Spellcasting Moon, and Solemn Echo Sparkle Incantation. Some of them involved matches and setting pieces of paper on fire, which Noora wouldn't let us do without her, for safety reasons, even though we are so so careful. A lot of them had to be done on special days, like the solstice or on a full moon, so they were kinda tricky to coordinate. But the easiest ones were where we mixed things into water then poured it in the garden while chanting certain words.

I'll never forget when one of the neighbors called Mom and warned her that we were "dancing around naked in the moonlight" one evening right before sunset. Mom immediately stormed out to the arroyo, still wearing her reading glasses and holding the red pen she uses for grading. The color of her face looked almost as red as the ink. But as soon as she discovered that we were in fact clothed and just dancing in a circle around a pile of lavender and mica-flecked stones we'd collected, her shoulders dropped down to their usual placement, and she broke out into a fit of chuckles.

Kayla's big grin appeared on her face. She flagged Mom over and motioned for us to make room in our moving circle for her. My mom skipped right over, joining our moving ritual as if she knew exactly what we were doing, waving her red pen in the air like a magic wand. "Some people are simply threatened by things they don't quite understand," she said after explaining why she'd approached us in such a rage.

I shake my head and Kayla rolls her eyes. "Our first spell was The Wishing Star Potion!" Her face lights up as she reminds me of all the different herbs we used, the moth wing we'd waited weeks to find because we couldn't bear the idea of killing a creature just for a spell, and the moon water in which we mixed all the ingredients. But my mind is elsewhere as we skip over roots and try to avoid taking a spill into the river. I'm trying to remember when I last saw the spell book. We had it at the tree house, and I remember Noora grabbing it. Where could she have dropped it?

"Remember we poured it onto your mom's tomato plants and she got so mad?" I shake my head and Kayla grabs onto the back of my shirt, causing me to fall backward into the ground.

"Hey!" All I can see is blue sky. The fall wouldn't have hurt so much if there weren't a million rocks there to break my fall. The biggest one is now digging into my hip.

Before I can push myself up into a seated position, Kayla's head comes into view as she peers over me. "I am so so sorry, are you OK?" she asks, her hands immediately grabbing mine and pulling too hard. Instead of landing on my feet, I fall forward into a chokeberry bush.

"I am so sorry, Ish," she says again, her eyebrows turning upwards like a cartoon. She reaches for my hand.

"Just don't pull so hard this time!" I laugh, then grab it anyway.

"I won't. Promise." She offers me a little smile, then asks, "You OK?"

"I'm just kind of weirded out still," I admit as I stand and brush dirt off my shorts. "You know, because of that feeling I had earlier." Kayla nods along with my words. I knew she'd get it. "And I really really want to find the spell book."

"Me too!" Kayla's eyes light up as she says it. "To do the Fluttering Heart spell."

We continue walking along the path in a single file line, Kayla in front this time, checking off every detail of the Fluttering Heart Charm spell. How long it takes to attract love: twenty-one days. The special ingredients involved in the spell: a cinnamon stick, a pink candle, and a piece of her crush's fingernail. In my head I'm still recounting our steps pre-rainstorm and thinking about the protection spell, but that last ingredient catches my attention.

"Wait, you need his fingernail? That's gross!"

"Spells require some weird things sometimes," she says, dodging the huge cholla spines sticking out into the path.

"I mean, how do you even get something like that? You'd have to go over to their house. No one trims their nails anywhere in public. At least no one worth crushing on."

Kayla just giggles, then quietly says, "Well, I already have it, so…" Her steps get faster to the point where she's practically speed-walking along the river.

Meanwhile, I've slowed down to a shuffle because my mind is churning. This spell is all she's talked about for days, but it never occurred to me that she'd actually go through with it. What happens if it actually works and she gets a boyfriend? I stop walking when it occurs to me: what if she finds someone to replace me?

"No way," I say under my breath, catching up with her. "Who is it? How have you never told me about him?!" This time I reach a hand out for her shirt. She spins around to face me and her cheeks are bright red.

"It's kinda a secret!"

"You have to tell me!" I shake my head in disbelief, but all she does is shake her head in response. "We're best friends, Kayla. More than best friends. Sissies." Between Noora leaving and Kayla acting so distant, it feels like our sisterhood is falling apart. After a long pause she finally speaks.

"I promise I will. Let's just find the spell book first." She says the words so fast, I barely have time to register what she's said. Before I know it, she's spun around and is already walking away from me.

I swallow hard, but the hurt leaves a metallic taste in my mouth. What is going on with Kayla? We never keep secrets from each other.

CHAPTER 21

(NOW)

I LEAN UP against the kitchen counter and try to gather my thoughts. All the previous cards were delivered right to my door. But this one has been sent to me via my sister's Instagram Stories. Barely a few minutes ago. My phone nearly dropped out of my hand when the image on Lulu's Instagram Story loaded. The card had the same teal border, frayed edges, and illustration aesthetic as the others. Whoever has been sending the cards has my sister. I'm sure of it now.

I pull up the screenshot I took of the Story, because who's to say how long it will stay up — and tabbing through all Lulu's other Stories featuring her smiling, cheery face to get to the card was far too gut-wrenching — but as soon as I see it bile rises up my throat. I've already determined that this card is the most haunting and terrifying one of the deck: Death. But that's not what has me worked up. It's what's on and around the card.

The whole card has been splattered with a viscous red liquid that looks undoubtedly like blood. Definitely blood. I stagger to the kitchen sink and retch into it. My stomach is completely empty, so nothing comes up, except for an onslaught of disturbing questions. Is that Lulu's blood? Is she alive still? Where do they have her? How do I even go about figuring out where she is?

There's no right place to start, so I just pick a place and begin. I check the local news sites, their social media accounts, and call nearby jails. But absolutely no leads. None of the local hospitals have had any patients come in with her name or description. So I widen my search, reaching out to anywhere within 100 miles of Rio Erizo. It's possible she could be farther than that by now.

Every dead end feels like a blow to my soul. I'm running out of both options and time.

I trudge to the bathroom, wash my face, then stare at my reflection in the mirror. My eyes look hollow and my complexion looks a little green, but it's my hair that's the most unsettling. My sleek chignon has unraveled and hangs lopsided over my right shoulder, the front pieces tangled and greasy. What an utterly perfect comparison to my life, which is coming undone as well.

But who am I to continue this pathetic pity party while my sister is out there, likely fighting for her life? My hands rise up and smack both of my cheeks, adding some pink to my green skin and snapping me out of my stupor. Now is not the time for doubt or despair. I remind myself, *This is what you do, Aisha. You analyze problems for a living.* Mind you, they're math problems, but it's still the same strategy. I will figure this out. I must.

I smooth my hair, then head to my office in order to prepare myself for the project. Looking at it as just another equation or problem and putting it at an arm's distance helps ease the nausea and unfurls the knot in my stomach just a bit. But not entirely.

My fingers pinch the screen to move the image and I begin evaluating it from the top left corner down the bottom right, moving it just a few millimeters at a time. Meanwhile, I take note of what sticks out in the background of the card: sand, twigs, broken pieces of cacti, ants, yucca, and pebbles. This could truly be anywhere in New Mexico.

The card features a knight on a horse holding a flag with XIII on it. Thirteen. *Thirteen thirteens are one hundred and sixty-nine.* But it's not a typical knight. This one is dead because I can clearly make out a skull under its armor rather than a human face. I use my fingers to zoom into the image and— How did I miss that before? My heartbeat quickens as I realize I missed a huge piece of the puzzle during my first several sweeps of the image. The message.

Handwritten words, nearly covered up by the red substance, flow from the skeleton's mouth. All the other cards had similar writing; how had I not thought to look for it? I shake my head and squeeze my eyes shut as I realize it's been quite a while since I've eaten. I'm not in the right mindset to solve this, but I have no choice. Lulu can't wait until I feel "just right." I take a deep breath in and continue on.

I can make out the first part of the message: "Endings whisper of what could—" but the rest is essentially illegible thanks to the blood covering it. Fortunately, I'm well-versed in extracting text from documents thanks to my colleagues' poor penmanship. In a matter of minutes, my program has nearly all of the message transcribed: "Endings whisper of what could have been. The sisters arcana race the unyielding hands of time as the clock's heartbeat grows quieter."

But along with the extracted text, I receive an error message. "Error 10C6: Some text could not be recognized." I zoom in as much as the program will let me and squint at the final word, trying to make it out.

Yes, I have most of the message and certainly enough to help me try to decode who could have Lulu, but something inside of me needs to know this final word. It may not make a difference, but I feel that tug. Is it anxiety or intuition? I don't know, but at this moment, I don't care. As the message says, we're at the mercy of the hands of time, and the clock is ticking, so the sooner I figure this out, the better.

The first letter is definitely H, followed by U, or maybe it's an O? I reverse the color scale but it doesn't seem to help. With a jolt of electric inspiration, I grab a notebook from my desk organizer and begin writing out every possible letter combination starting with the letter H. It's not numbers, but I still feel right at home solving this equation.

"Hurt?" Is Lulu hurt? Panic tightens in my chest at the thought. Maybe "hurst," meaning she's in a forest? "Hostage?" She's certainly been taken hostage, but what would the sender accomplish by writing that? It only takes a few more guesses before my pen scrawls out my best possible guesstimate.

"Hurry."

* * *

"So you say she's been missing for four hours?" The operator's slow, monotone voice leads me to believe that he isn't taking me seriously. That, or he hates his job, which could certainly be the case. "That's really not very long."

"Maybe not," I grip the phone in my hand tighter, "but there was the disturbing Instagram Story with all the blood." I already mentioned this detail, but it's worth saying again.

"What's her handle again?"

"L-U-M-double A-R-A-3-3-3."

"Hmmm, I'm not seeing it."

"Did you remember the double As?"

"Yeah, I mean, I'm on her profile and I see her Stories but not that one…" he says.

"No effing way," I breathe. Of course. They deleted it. I drop my head onto the desk then yell into the phone, "Wait, I have a screenshot of it!"

"Ma'am, that doesn't really matter," he replies in that same monotone. "If it doesn't show her in explicit danger, it doesn't warrant investigation—"

"Yet," I interrupt.

"Sure, *yet*, plus, she hasn't been missing long enough to send out a search team." His speech has picked up in speed. I can tell he's getting annoyed with me.

"What about a wellness check?" I plead, my voice cracking.

"Sure, we can do that," he sighs. "Within the next few hours, expect an officer to stop by to check on—"

"Wait, a few hours?" I simply can't wait that long. I pull my phone away from my ear and faintly hear the operator continue speaking, but I don't register what he's saying. *Three hours. One hundred and eighty minutes. Thirty-two thousand and four hundred.*

She could be dead by then. If she isn't already. I tap the End button on my phone and stuff it into my back pocket. I'm running out of options. There's only one thing left to do.

CHAPTER 22

(NOW)

My phone dings and I take a quick glance at the notification.

Your Uber driver, Iris, has arrived.

It's been almost six hours since my sister went dark and my anxiety has escalated exponentially since taking this next step. My breath becomes shallow and the fingers on my right hand instinctively find the top of my head. Tap, tap, tap, tap. I press the pads of my fingers into the crown of my head in a repetitive motion as I say, "It's OK to be scared, I just need my courage to outweigh my fear."

I tend to reserve EFT tapping for times of extreme stress, like this. And right now, I'm willing to have a go at anything that can provide me with even a sliver of relief as I take on this huge endeavor. I lift the inside of my other wrist up to my nose and take a deep inhale of the lavender oil I'd dabbed there earlier as I continue tapping. Another calming technique. My affirmations are listed out in my notes app and several meditation tracks are downloaded and ready to play should I need them. I'm prepared to quell any stressful storms that might try to knock me off balance.

But before I can even work my way to tapping the fourth meridian — the side of the eye — my phone rings. I squeeze my eyes shut and bring the phone in front of me. But when I open my eyes, my hunch is confirmed. Instead of seeing Lulu's name across my screen, it reads "Maybe Iris."

"I'll be right out!" I shout into the phone, then tuck it into my pocket and grab my backpack. Inside is anything and everything I could possibly need out in the outside world. Being prepared for all contingencies is the only way I can survive this. I haul the bag over my shoulder then open the front door.

As soon as I take the first step over the threshold, I'm bombarded with sounds, sights, and smells. A brisk breeze dances through the patches of tall grasses aesthetically arranged along the path from my front door to the street, bringing with it the heavenly scent of honeysuckle. Light shines through the cottonwoods, creating a dappled pattern of shadows on the ground in front of me. Everything is intensified out here. Even the chirps of the birds that I've only heard from inside my home feel overwhelming.

Within mere seconds, my head seems like it detaches from my body and starts to float up toward the bright blue New Mexican sky. Instead of allowing my eyes to follow it, I force my gaze down to the ground. *Stay grounded, Aisha.* I grip the straps of my backpack tighter and tighter, my short nails digging into the soft flesh of my palms through the canvas material.

One step at a time, I remind myself.

I take a deep breath and focus on my feet. *Two, three, four, five.* My Mary Janes shuffle along the flagstone path toward the sidewalk as my mind battles between hope and fear. *I can do it, I am doing it! Thirteen and fourteen.* Before I know it, I'm standing on the curb in front of Iris' station wagon.

"Well, hi there, darlin'."

Upon opening the back door, Iris turns around in the front seat and gives me a big wave. She's wearing a surgical mask, but I can tell she's smiling under it based on the cheer in her voice and the way her eyes crinkle at the corners. Her hair is the same deep purple shade you'd see on an iris, while her cat-eye frames are a hot pink. Like a Barbie pink. On most people the two colors would clash horribly or make them look juvenile, but on this woman, they totally work.

Something shimmery behind her catches my eye and I have to squint to make it out. A bedazzled name plate sitting on her dashboard reads "Iris" in big, sparkly letters.

I poke my head in and whisper through my surgical mask, "Are you Iris?" I can't be too sure. It's possible my sister's captor sent someone to abduct me, so I won't let my guard down.

She lets out a hearty laugh that practically shakes the entire car then points to the nameplate. "The one and only."

I keep my feet planted on the sidewalk and glance down the street, just to confirm no one is watching me. A neighbor four doors down, someone I don't recognize and have probably never seen before because I can't see them from my window, is sitting on their balcony, chatting on the phone while painting their nails. *Four fours are...*

My front door is right there. The sight of its vibrant turquoise paint and the little ristra hanging above the peephole cause a warm sensation to spread through my belly and chest. It's safe in there. I could be back in my living room in as little as fourteen steps. Probably eight if I take big leaps. *Eight eights are sixty-four...*

"You ready, little lady?" She raises an eyebrow and pushes her glasses up the bridge of her nose. "Somethin' you needed to do before we leave?"

"No, no," I reply. "Just a little nervous is all." I look down at my gloved hands and can see the condensation forming underneath the latex from my perspiration. But it's better than exposing myself to bacteria and any viruses lingering out in the world. Germs aren't one of my biggest fears, per se, but I haven't been outside in years. A whole pandemic has transpired in those years, so I'll take all the protection I can get.

"Oooooh," she says, drawing out the O far longer than is necessary, but not in a condescending way. There's an undertone of understanding. Like she gets it.

"If it makes you feel any better," Iris explains as she reaches forward into her glove compartment, "I sanitize the whole car after each ride." She presents a package of wipes, then quickly adds, "My daughter has OCD, so I'm no stranger to phobias, although I certainly don't want to assume that's what's going on here. But just know, I see you."

My shoulders fall a bit. I do feel seen. I give her a quick nod then take a step into the car and settle in, placing my backpack on my feet, keeping my tight grasp on the strap. I have twelves fresh pairs of gloves in case I need them. *Twelve twelves are...* I squeeze my eyes shut and quickly shake my head back and forth.

"Don't want to startle you, ma' dear." My eyes shoot open. Iris' voice is now coming from outside of the car; she's standing there looking down on me with a hand on the door. "Just going to shut this and we'll be on our way."

The door. *Effity eff!* "I'm so sorry, it's just been a while—"

I start explaining, but Iris is already back in the driver's seat, waving me off with her right hand as she types into her phone with the left.

"No need to apologize, darlin'. We'll be there in twenty-two minutes." She turns and looks at me again. "But I'll let you know if that changes so you can plan accordingly." I'd hoped my driver would be one of the silent, stoic types, but there's something about Iris that puts me at ease. Maybe it's her quirky appearance or the way the word "darlin'" drips off her tongue like warm maple syrup.

"Thank you," I whisper. "I think that's where I need to go, but I really have no idea what I'm doing." I notice Iris' eyebrow raise, but she doesn't say anything.

On second thought, I don't want to get too comfortable with Iris. I'm not entirely sure I can trust her yet. Or anyone, for that matter.

CHAPTER 23

(THEN)

SHE WON'T EVEN look at me now. Every time I try to catch up with Kayla, she just walks faster, and the handful of times that I've tried to make conversation, she just pretends she doesn't hear me. All I did was ask about her crush! If anyone should be annoyed, it's me. She tells me everything, and this feels like a pretty big secret.

But I do have bigger things to worry about right now. Like finding the spell book. I'm about to take on the role of big sister and Lulu will be relying on me. That's why I need to do this protection spell. I lift my head up a little higher and move my feet a little quicker along the patch, kicking up loose dirt and leaves.

Kayla turns left at the two baby ponderosa pines and begins hiking up toward the trail to the tree house. I glance at my

Spice Girls watch and check the time. It's almost 6:30 pm. So much for a shortcut! The bumpy terrain along the river definitely slowed us down, but at least we still have some time to search for the book before we have to head home. Noora said to be on the street by eight, and I'll get us back by then. *With* the spell book. If Kayla hadn't pulled me down or made such a big deal about her stupid crush spell, we might already be at the tree house.

Just as the ground changes from rocks to soft sand, I hear a grunt. My head whips around but I try to keep my body perfectly still. I even hold my breath to avoid making a peep. I see a glimpse of blue from behind a mass of salt cedar branches. There's something there. Or someone. I strain my eyes to get a better look through the trees. It moves again and I squint even more. *I've got you this time…*

"Aisha!" Kayla's voice breaks my concentration and causes me to jump. "Are you coming?" I snap my gaze from Kayla's red face back to the spot, but the blue is gone.

"Ish?"

My head rotates slowly from the salt cedar, meeting Kayla's pleading eyes with my glaring ones. "Would you just be quiet for a second?" My heart is beating so fast it feels like it might explode in my chest.

Kayla's shoulders round and her whole body deflates. "I'm just trying to help," she whispers.

"But you're not!" The words come out sounding a lot angrier than I mean them to, and I can tell I've really hurt Kayla's feelings. My fists start to ball up like Lulu's do when she's mad. It feels good to squeeze them tight, imagining that all the anger in my body is in my palms and I'm squeezing it until it turns into something good. Like how we learned in science you can squeeze carbon with such force that it creates a diamond.

I don't want to be upset with Kayla — we hardly ever fight — but I'm feeling pretty hurt myself. I give the branches a long last look — the blue is totally gone by now and I don't spot anything else moving in the trees — then huff past her and start marching up the slope.

"What has gotten into you?" Her sad voice is right behind me but she feels light-years away.

"I feel so out of the loop with your life. Like, do I even know you?"

She grabs my hand from behind, pulling me to a stop. "Of course you know me. We're sissies. Always have been, always will be."

"I just don't understand why you kept this secret from me! I tell you everything!" More than that, I just don't have time for her drama. My big sister is leaving for college and I won't see her again until Thanksgiving. I'll need to be Mom's second in command. Kayla has both of her parents and has never had a sibling leave. She doesn't know what it feels like to be abandoned. I stare up at the cottonwood leaves fluttering against the blue sky to keep the tears in my eyes.

"Are you trying to replace me?" I ask quietly.

"That's ridiculous!"

"Shhhhh, you're being so loud!"

"I don't care!" Kayla shouts even louder, taking several big steps so she's right in front of me. The whites of her eyes are now almost as red and splotchy as her face. I can see her blinking back tears, but I don't know if they're because she's hurt or because the winds are picking up.

"And clearly you don't care about me anymore." I take a step back and cross my arms.

"Of course, I do! You're going to be the first person I tell, I just need to find the spell book first."

"What does it matter if it's after we find the book or before? Just tell me!" I throw my hands up in the air to make my point.

"Fine, Ish. If you must know… it's you." She breaks eye contact and looks down at the ground, her voice lowering down to a whisper. "I wanted to do the spell on you."

Before I even have a chance to process it, Kayla turns on her heels and races back down toward the river path, leaving me standing there alone. And completely stunned.

CHAPTER 24

(NOW)

DRIVING THROUGH RIO ERIZO feels a bit like a dream with its adobe homes and sloping mountains as the backdrop, probably because I find myself walking through these streets most nights while I sleep. It has been so long since I stepped foot out of my house. Yes, I've cherished the solitude and safety it provides, but at the same time I've longed to break free from its shackles. I just didn't think it would ever be possible. Yet, here I am, driving toward my old neighborhood.

I expected the confined car to make me feel more anxious, but it's actually kind of a relief. I feel somewhat in control in here. Protected, at least. I gaze out the window while we're stopped at a streetlight and watch as a pair of women stroll along the sidewalk. Their arms are linked, the summer wind whispering through their hair. One must have made a joke because the other clutches her stomach and doubles over in laughter. My heart rate slows a little and I feel a warmth spread across my chest as I watch them, longing for what they have. I wonder if Lulu and I will ever have an opportunity to take a walk and share a moment like that.

You never will. I can feel the intrusive thoughts start making their way back into my mind, seeping into the cracks like water into a leaky roof. Looking at a photo of Lulu or watching one of her Reels might help me stay focused. At least it'll remind me why I'm making this journey. Journeying so far out of my comfort zone. My gloved fingers awkwardly navigate my back pocket as I work to wiggle my phone out, my eyes still staring out the window.

"They look happy, huh?" Iris' voice cuts through the silence. She's turned around in her seat and is looking right at me, the light in front of us still shining a bright, ominous red.

I momentarily meet her gaze then glance down at my phone, embarrassed that she caught me staring at those women. "Yeah, they do…" is all I can get out because as my phone comes to life from my touch, "Lumaara333 added to their story" sits at the top of my lock screen.

The photo was posted just four minutes ago. *Four fours are sixteen. Two hundred and fifty-six.* We have to hurry or it might be too late. This new image shows the same scene as the last, but instead of including The Death tarot card, I can make out a corner of Lulu's woven skirt.

The one she was wearing yesterday.

The image is blurry, as if the phone is moving. Maybe they're forcing her to walk through this whole ordeal? I force the bile back down my throat. I don't want to imagine what kind of twisted games they're playing with her, but my mind goes there anyway. I see her being led to the edge of a cliff, sobbing and pleading as she's forced to walk over the cliffside. Next, I imagine her being used as a sacrifice in some kind of dark, evil ritual. In another scenario she's hung from a tree next to the tire swing and…

NO! I drop my phone into my lap, placing both my hands over my ears, then shake my head with such force that my neck begins to throb. I cannot let these thoughts get to me. I need to focus.

I grab my phone and zoom in on the latest Story. I've already noted Lulu's skirt. The direction of her shadow indicates that it's midafternoon, so it was likely just taken and isn't an old photo. There's what looks like ponderosas in the background — it's difficult to see because of the photo quality, but I recognize the shape of the branches. But what's that in front of the smallest ponderosa pine? It looks like keys hanging off it? I zoom in closer, trying to make out details when it hits me. Not a key. An earring.

This changes everything. She's not at Dr. Wiley's, as I'd initially guessed. She's somewhere far more intimate and secluded.

"Iris?" My voice comes out as just a squeak. "Instead of the address I plugged into the app, I need you to take me a little farther down the street." I lean forward and show her the map on my phone, pointing to the spot I'm almost certain they are. "Here."

"Sure thing, darlin'." With a nod she pulls over and plugs the location into her GPS. "Rerouting!" Iris makes the announcement like she's a train conductor. "Be there in less than a minute."

"We're here," Iris says as she pulls over to the side of the road.

Cactus Creek. Even through the veil of overwhelm I recognize it like the back of my hand. There's the opening in the trees that descends down into the arroyo toward the tree house. Still, it's a bit fancier than it was almost two decades ago — the opening in the trees has become a true trailhead with a big sign boasting "Cactus Creek Trail," a community board, and the cherry on top: a doggy poop bag dispenser. There's even a map of the trail network, something that looks a little like the one we created ourselves as kids.

This is it. I feel something stir in my chest. It's not fear or anxiety, which is usually what I feel there. Instead, I think it's pride. I can't believe I'm out here in the real world attempting to find my sister. The tears start dripping off my chin before I even feel them leave my eyes. I unzip my backpack and rifle through it, but I already know I failed to pack tissues. Disinfecting wipes, yes. Gloves, tons. A pair of safety goggles, not one, but two. But no tissues. Crying wasn't even on my radar. I was focused more on threats from the outside rather than the ones inside of me, like my emotions.

Through my misty eyes, I spot a figure pacing back and forth at the mouth of the trail. Their deliberate, graceful gait immediately makes me think of Lulu's flowy hands while she pulls tarot cards. She's even wearing a flowy skirt that reminds me of Lulu's. Wait, no, it can't be. My hand goes to my chest. Is that her?

I'd expected to be confronted by her captor and… well, I'm not entirely sure what I'd expected, but the possibilities were endless. And mostly life threatening. Maybe I'd have to put up a fight, physically or verbally, offer a ransom for her safe return, or plead for mercy.

I reach toward the car door handle but barely graze it before I pull my hand back. This has to be a trap. They're watching her, using her as bait. My palms become sweaty and I feel the bile begin to rise up my throat at the thought. With her determined steps and calm face, she doesn't look frightened. But I imagine she is deep down. My brave Lulu. She was always so good at stuffing her emotions down as a child. It's clear she still is.

"You alright there?" Iris breaks the silence once again and I'm transported back to the present. As the tarot card said, the clock's heartbeat grows quieter, which means I need to act quickly. My fingers find the crown of my head and begin tapping. Don't think about it, just do it.

"Iris." My voice comes out sounding far braver than I feel. "I need you to wait here for me."

"Sure thing, darlin'," she replies, her eyes smiling underneath those quirky glasses. "I wasn't going to leave until I knew you were OK anyway, what with that guy wandering around."

My eyes follow her chin as she nods toward a man walking down the sidewalk. My throat starts to tighten as soon as I focus in on the figure striding in Lulu's direction. He's no longer wearing the beanie, but I know it's him. My instinct was right. He's watching Lu, waiting for me. I need to hurry. But before I can even get the door open he's already behind my sister. He reaches his hand up the back of her top, then nuzzles her neck.

In mere seconds I'm out the door, grabbing my backpack at I leap out of the car. I'm moving as quickly as my body will allow me, but the scene appears to unfold in slow motion. Lulu turns around, her hand flying through the air toward his face. *Hit him hard, Lu!* I cheer in my head. Her hand makes contact with his cheek — but it's a caress. And now her lips are on his.

I feel my heart freeze over and I stop in my tracks.

What the eff is going on?

CHAPTER 25

(THEN)

THIS CANNOT BE happening. I stop running for a second to catch my breath. My hands find my knees as the burning moves from my chest to my throat. After Kayla took off, it took me a few minutes to sort out my thoughts and go after her. *Wait, me? Me. She likes me.* How had I not seen it before?

But now I can't find her anywhere. I retrace my steps back to where she dropped the huge bomb, keeping an eye out for her neon green Limited Too t-shirt and denim jorts — the outfit she'd borrowed from me after getting drenched in the rain just hours before. It shouldn't be this hard to spot. She must be hiding really well. That or she's already made it back home.

"Sissy! Kayla! Kayla?" My voice echoes down the river and my feet follow.

Where is she? I pause for a second, then close my eyes and

put my hands on my heart. What is my intuition telling me? The thoughts in my head are so loud, I simply can't hear it today. I shake my head a little, trying to clear things and shake my intuition to the surface, but nothing happens. "Blegh." I throw my hands by my side and keep walking. Things will clear up soon, I just need to keep moving.

As I work my way down the river's edge, I spot some perfect skipping stones. Exactly like the ones Kayla taught me to look for. I bend over to pick one up, smiling as I rub my thumb along the smooth surface. It was down here that Kayla taught me how to skip stones.

"You need to get really low," she'd told me, hinging at her hips until her upper body was almost level with the water. "Then throw it sideways," she explained. "Like this."

The flat stone sailed perfectly through the air, skipping not once or twice but four times. "Woohooo!" I shouted, jumping up and down until she joined me, our stone-filled fists raised up high above us.

"Now you try." I tried to put my body in the same position and loaded up my arm just like she had, but when I released the skipping stone, it just plunked right into the water. "It's OK, Sissy, try again." She smiled and handed me one of her stones. The weight of it felt comforting in my palm. Just as Kayla's presence always made me feel at ease.

"Kayla, can we just talk about it, please?" I shout down the river again, holding my stone-filled fists up to my mouth to make my voice louder. We learned in science class that making a funnel like that really does amplify your voice. And I want my voice to carry as far as possible so Kayla can hear me.

I'm not sure what I'll say when I finally do see her, though. I stop and drop all but one of my perfect skipping stones on the water's edge, prepare myself in my perfect skipping posture, and let the stone fly. One, two, three skips. Not too shabby, especially since the water is moving a lot more today than usual.

Maybe something like, "I love you so so much, Kayla, just not in a romantic way?" or "Kayla, I care about you so much and meant it when I said we'd be friends forever, but I just don't have the same romantic feelings?" She's my best friend and my favorite person in the world, but I don't get the warm fuzzies in my belly when I look at her the way I do when I look at the poster of Nick Carter on my bedroom door. She'll understand, and we can go back to the way things were before. At least I hope so.

"Ugh!" I shout at the water. I toss my remaining stones in as well, then continue marching in the direction of the street. My feet start to sink into the wet sand with every step. I need to keep moving or I'll slide in. As I walk, Kayla's confession replays in my head. *I wanted to do the spell on you.*

I wish I hadn't pushed her to tell me who her crush was! Everything would be fine if I hadn't. We'd have the book by now, I'd be on my way to doing the protection spell on Lulu, and Kayla would be doing her spell. Oh, who am I kidding? I kick a big pile of sand with as much force as I can muster. I'd find out about her crush at some point, and we'd be in the same situation we are now.

Suddenly, I see a glint of neon green peeking out from behind a tamarisk. "Kayla!" I cry, happy to have finally found her. But as I get closer, I see that something is wrong. Very wrong.

CHAPTER 26

(NOW)

The afternoon casts long shadows over the well-trod ground of the trailhead. Typically, this is the time that hikers would be coming back to their cars after a jaunt in the arroyo, but that's not always the case in New Mexico. Golden hour is prime time for photographs, so there are several people just arriving. I spot a few couples, quinceañeras, and influencers, but I have my eyes fixed on one specific influencer, though she doesn't seem to notice me. Yet.

"What the eff is going on?"

My voice snaps my sister and her captor out of their steamy make out session. Beanie dude pulls his hands off her and staggers backward, giving me that same shocked look I'd seen on his face through the window.

"Who are you?" I hiss through my mask, taking a few

hesitant steps toward him. But Lulu inserts herself between us before I can reach him. She reaches for my gloved hand but I quickly pull it back. She's right in front of me but it feels like we're miles apart. Is she in on this? What on Earth is happening?

"It's not what you think—" he starts, but she interrupts him.

"No, let me tell her." He retreats like a puppy with his tail between his legs. I'd thought she was the one in danger, but the way she speaks to this man makes it look like she's the one in charge.

"Tell me what?" I have an idea of what is going on here, but I don't want to believe it just yet. Not until I have all the facts. "What is going on, and who are you?"

"Ish," Lulu says, her voice adopting that soft breathy quality from her videos, like she's about to tell me something I don't quite want to hear. But need to.

"This is my husband, Nate."

I stare at Lulu in disbelief. She's known this man all along, the one lurking in my backyard and the one who abducted her? No, not just known. She is married to him! I'd been so convinced she was in danger but here she is, holding hands with this man. Lulu was in my home. We talked — caught up. But not once did she mention she was married.

My mind races with a million questions, though one burns brighter than the others. Before I can open my mouth, Lulu continues. "I know this is a lot to take in, but there's so much I have to tell you."

A warm, wet pressure blooms on my leg and I look down to see a red heeler sniffing at my pants, their nose buried in the seams. The hiker attached to the other end of the leash pulls on it gently, trying to steer away from our tense conversation.

I wish I could retreat, too, but I need clarity. I hinge over and give the pup a quick pat on the head.

"So start talking," I reply, still gazing into the heeler's comforting eyes.

"Um, OK." Lulu shifts her weight and wrings her hands. I would have expected her to have something prepared. What did she think? That I was just going to be OK with her going missing, and then reappearing without an explanation? But I suppose that's the difference between us. Maybe we're not as connected as I'd begun to think.

"Well, we've just been so worried about you, and you need to understand this was all done out of love." She's speaking quickly, her eyes bouncing from the poop bag dispenser to the bench, a tree, then another, but never meeting my gaze. Wow, I don't think I've ever seen Lulu so agitated. Even as a child she was so incredibly calm.

The dog owner is now chatting with a friend, so I still have my gloved fingers twirled in the pooch's wavy tresses. "What's your name, buddy?" I whisper close to his ear, then locate the tag hanging from his collar. It reads "BLAZE" with a tiny flame emoji. *Of course*, I think, letting out a sputtery chuckle. *Of course Blaze is following me.*

"…and we knew you wouldn't leave otherwise. We've been so worried knowing you were confined to that little townhouse, but—"

My brain starts to buzz, and I snap my body upright.

"Wait, let me get this straight — you orchestrated all of this?" She nods slowly.

"A-And the cards? You…" The weight of the realization presses on my chest. I can't breathe. I'm caught in a spiral of emotion — confusion, anger, hopelessness, and denial. How could she do this to me? Force me into this state of anxiety?

"I promise you, it was for a very good reason." Her eyes are filled with pleading and her nose is a rosy pink. I see the little Lulu in there.

"Really?" I scoff. "If it's so good, tell me what it is."

"I can't." The tears start to tumble down her cheeks. "You just have to trust me."

I want to believe my sister, but how can I? How can I trust her after she's betrayed me like this? I turn on my heels, striding back in the direction of Iris' car. Relief washes over my body when I see it still there. *Thank you, Iris!* But it's a short-lived relief.

"Wait," I say softly, stopping in my tracks and spinning around to face Lulu. "You keep saying 'we.'" I look from Lulu to Nate, then back again. "Does that mean you two were worried and did all of this, or is this 'we' you and someone else?"

Lulu tilts her head to the side, looking me straight in the eye. Her voice comes out breathy again. "Someone else was helping me," she starts.

"Who?" I snap back, looking toward Nate. There can't be more, this is more than enough for one day. A figure emerges from behind the trees at the mouth of the trail, and my knees buckle.

No effing way.

CHAPTER 27

(THEN)

FINGERS OF SALT cedar grasp Kayla's ankle and the spell book floats next to her in the water. The gentle waves lap at her skin, like they're patting her cheeks — but instead of a pretty pink color like usual, they're gray. Still, she looks so peaceful, like she's sleeping. But I know she's not.

Panic pulses through me and every fiber in my body is screaming at me to move. To reach down and shake Kayla. To yell at her and try to force her awake. To pull her out of the water, but my feet are glued to the ground. I can't move. All I can do is stare at my best friend and hope that someone else stumbles on us.

My wish is granted when I see a figure running down the trail. But it's the last person I want to see. *Get away from my Sissy,* I want to scream, but it's too late. He's already in front of her, wrapping his fingers around her wrists and dragging her out of the water.

I haven't been this close to Dr. Wiley in years, not since I last saw him for an exam when I was a baby. Like, five or six years old. Since then, he's definitely changed. He always looks messy and freaked out, like he's running away from something. Mom says it's his mind, but who would want that badly to get away from themselves?

As Dr. Wiley looks down at Kayla's lifeless body, I expect to see that wild, frantic look in his eyes, but it's not there. Instead, his eyes are filled with kindness. His eyebrows turn downward like he's worried, but his hands don't show it. They move like lightning.

He places two fingers on Kayla's neck, then lifts her chin up a bit, putting his ear down toward her mouth. I think I see his head shake for a second because he then goes right for her chest. *One, two, three, four.* I count as Dr. Wiley presses his palms into her chest with so much force I'm worried he's hurting her.

Don't hurt her! I want to scream, but all that escapes my lips is a gurgling noise. I blink over and over, hoping that maybe I'm seeing things wrong. Am I dreaming? Maybe I'm the one that needs to wake up, not my best friend.

Dr. Wiley keeps pushing on Kayla's chest, but he must have heard my sound because his eyes are on me now. I see his mouth move as if he's speaking to me, but all I can hear is my heart beating in my ears. How is this happening?

The ache in my ears moves down my body until it's concentrated in my heart. It feels as though it's been ripped out of my own chest and is being smashed like Kayla's is right now. But I can't look away.

I see Dr. Wiley pause, then give two quick breaths into her mouth before going back to compressions, like what we learned about in health class. He speaks again and this time I can make out what he's saying.

"Come on, Miss Kayla. Come back," he grunts. Then he turns back to me. "Are you keeping time?"

I glance down at my watch. The long hand points to Sporty Spice now, meaning it's 7:30 — Noora is going to kill me for being late, and the sun is barely visible between the cottonwood trees. But I don't have time to think about that.

"Two minutes," Dr. Wiley says again in response to my gaping mouth. I give a quick nod, then nod again when time is up. He must understand my signal because he stops, gives Kayla two more breaths, then continues the pattern.

We keep going, and between compressions, Dr. Wiley talks to Kayla, telling her to "stay with us" and "keep fighting." He also mutters to himself, saying things like "…what I get for trying to avoid running into anyone… they'll never believe me if I tried to explain…no one respects energy healing these days…" None of his mumbles seem like they're meant for me, so I keep my eyes fixed on the second hand ticking on my wrist.

At least I'm doing something now — actually helping instead of just standing there. I'm not sure how long we go for, but Dr. Wiley doesn't stop, and neither do I.

I don't stop timing or hoping Kayla will come back.

"Do something!"

I spin my head to see Marie standing there, staring at me. Where did she come from? I look behind Marie to see if anyone else is with her, but she's alone. How did she find us? My focus snaps to her dark brown eyes and the fear radiating through them. I want to explain everything and tell her I'm so so sorry, but I'm still frozen.

"He's hurting her! Why aren't you doing anything?" she shouts again, pointing at Dr. Wiley and Kayla. But I can't. I still can't move no matter how much determination I put into my legs. Marie does what I can't do and runs head-on toward them.

"Stop it!" she shouts, trying to push Dr. Wiley out of the way. He's so much bigger than her and, even though he's panting and sweating, he could still easily shove Marie off to the side. He doesn't, though. Instead, he checks for Kayla's pulse. He then tries to keep his own ragged breath still as he brings his ear close to her motionless chest, then hangs his head. We've been at it for almost an hour. Kayla is gone.

Dr. Wiley backs up to give Marie space, and she instantly falls to her knees on the riverbank and buries her face in Kayla's neck. The sun is long gone by now, but the full moon creates a creepy glow over the whole scene. I can make out Marie's tiny body over Kayla's but it's her cries that tug at my heart.

"Wake up, Sissy! Everything is going to be OK," she sobs into Kayla's wet hair, strands clinging to both of their cheeks.

I squeeze my eyes shut and wish I hadn't seen them like that — Kayla's limp body and Marie struggling to lift her. But the image is imprinted in my mind. I shake my head gently like I'm shaking my Etch A Sketch to clear the picture, but it just won't go away. My head shakes faster and faster, until I get dizzy. All I want is my friend back. To rewind, before everything turned to chaos.

I look to Dr. Wiley, who is nearly completely swallowed by the darkness, but my attention is quickly pulled to the trees' edge where Noora and Lulu burst through.

"We've been looking for you all over!" Lulu's voice pierces through my skull and shakes me from my foggy trance. She gallops over to me and wraps her arms around my waist, but it still feels like everything is happening in slow motion.

"Are you OK? Why are you so la—" Noora starts as she scans the scene, but when her eyes fall on Kayla and Marie, her eyes widen and she lets out a scream. "What happened?" she shrieks, running over to the girls. Just as she'd done with Dr. Wiley, Marie pushes Noora away, her desperate sobs echoing off the water like an animal's cries.

Noora returns to my side, her eyes pleading for an explanation, but I have none. I try to move my mouth but I feel like I'm yelling through water. Finally, I look back to Dr. Wiley, but he's already gone.

"It's OK, it's fine. Don't worry," Noora says, more to herself it seems that to any of us. Her hands tremble as she fishes around in her tie-dye fanny pack. "I have the emergency phone. It's going to be OK. Everything's OK…"

I desperately hope it will be OK, but it sure doesn't feel like it.

"Mom will be here in ten minutes and said not to move a muscle," Noora says in a quiet voice. "And the police should be right behind her."

We're standing in the dark now, using the emergency phone — Mom's slim Motorola Razor — to flag down the adults when they get here and as a flashlight to keep an eye on Marie. She hasn't left Kayla's side and hasn't stopped crying.

Noora has kept Lulu behind me so she can't see anything. Although I don't know if that will be much help. She definitely saw Kayla's body. I know the image is going to be branded in my brain for the rest of my life — I expect the same will be true for Lu.

"I'm scared." Lulu hasn't let go of me and I can feel her small body shivering in the cool evening air. Noora reaches her arms around both of us and gives us a big hug.

"It's OK, Sissies. Why don't we do something to distract ourselves?" She always knows exactly what to do. "What are you learning in school?" Her eyes bounce between the two of us, but I have no words. Only panic. My brain is beginning to thaw out and I'm feeling everything that has happened.

Finally, Lulu says, "Multiplication tables."

"Perfect! Let's do some of those together." Noora grabs both of our hands and squeezes them. "What's five times five?"

"Twenty-five," Lulu replies.

"Good! Now six times six?"

As Lulu grips my waist tighter and tighter, I try to repeat the numbers, but I can't stop thinking about the whole thing — Kayla's confession, Kayla running off, finding her, and Dr. Wiley showing up. Right before he vanished, I saw him bring a finger up to his mouth as if to say "shhh," and all I could do was nod. I keep shaking my head to shake away the image, wondering if it was supposed to be a warning or support. At least me and the doc were somewhat on the same wavelength. If our parents knew he was here, they'd definitely be mad.

I can keep his secret, if he doesn't tell anyone what I did — which was nothing. Absolutely nothing.

CHAPTER 28

(NOW)

NO MATTER HOW wide I open my eyes, I still can't believe who is standing in front of me. She looks just as I remember her, though a little older and even more elegant. Her tall frame is draped in a pale peach suit — both the jacket and pants are slightly oversized in a trendy and intentional way, as if they were made to fit her exact measurements. And knowing what she does for a living, I expect they likely were custom made. A delicate gold chain trickles down her throat, which her fingers won't leave alone. She's methodically twisting and untwisting the necklace as she looks at me expectantly. Still that same nervous energy, just wrapped up in designer clothing.

"Hey, Sissy." Noora steps in front of Lulu and frees her hand from her necklace long enough to give me a small wave. Memories flood my mind — joyful ones, painful ones, and everything in between. Saturday morning walks to the library with our arms weighed down by books to return and our mouths filled with musings about our favorite characters.

We spent so much time together as children. I idolized my big sister, but we haven't spoken since she left for college, right after the accident. Yes, we saw each other at holidays and family gatherings, but the few words she spoke to me were always just superficial pleasantries. We lost touch, and it left a gaping hole in my heart.

Noora steps toward me and gently says, "Aisha, we hope you understand that we were just trying to help."

I just stand there gaping at my sisters. It's laughable really, and before I realize what I'm doing, a chuckle erupts from my mouth. I'm laughing with my head back, hands on my stomach. I can't remember the last time I belly-laughed like this, although it was probably with my sisters. Certainly not under the same circumstances, though.

"Help?" I finally sputter between laughs. "You think this was helpful?" My eyes dart back and forth between the two of them. "Leaving cryptic messages at my doorstep, forcing me into a spiral of panic and paranoia, worming your way into my life, pretending to be in danger," I jab a finger at Lulu, "and forcing me to leave my home far before I was ready?" I stand there in utter disbelief, looking at my two sisters. Who do these women think they are? They're not caring, compassionate sisters, that's for sure. They have manipulated and gaslit me beyond my wildest fears.

"And you," I point at Noora, my voice rising and shaking with rage. "Why show up now, after all this time?" She looks away, tugging again on her necklaces. "I know you've been in Rio Erizo this entire time," I hiss. I pause for a moment to catch my breath but neither of them says a word. "Why concoct this insane scheme instead of reaching out to me directly?"

"We thought this would—" Lulu says quickly, looking to Noora. My blood boils at that small action. How pathetic of me to feel as though I needed to be Lulu's protector. She's had our big sissy on her side the entire time.

"What? Gain my trust? *Fix* me?" I spit the words out with so much venom that even I'm surprised. I can tell my sisters are taken aback by the way Noora's eyebrows shoot up. *Yeah, go ahead and write that in your ledger, or whatever a psychiatrists' notebook is called.*

I turn around and walk toward my Uber, though this time I don't turn back despite Lulu and Noora's pleas. "We love you so much," Lulu keeps saying, her breathy voice cracking with desperation. "We want what's best for you." "Just give us a minute." "We know you better than you know yourself." That last one stings, though I keep walking with determination, willing my legs to not shake quite so visibly. I don't want them to know how hurt I am.

Finally, I collapse in the back seat of Iris' car, her calming energy enveloping me like a big hug. "Everything alright?" she inquires delicately, taking a peek at me in the rear view but not turning her body around as she'd done before. Even Iris is more in tune with me and my moods than my own sisters.

"Fine," I reply shortly. "Could you drop me back at home, please?"

"Sure thing, darlin'. We'll be there in nineteen minutes."

Nineteen nineteens are three hundred and sixty-one. I close my eyes and let the numbers caress my vibrating brain.

CHAPTER 29

(NOW)

THE LAST THREE days have blurred together as a foggy haze of baking, eating, and cleaning, then repeating the cycle over and over and over again. But even with my belly full of warm banana bread, my heart remains emptier than ever, and my head spins with paranoia.

They're incredibly persistent, I'll give them that. My sisters have called me incessantly for the past three days. *Three threes are nine, eighty-one, six thousand five hundred and sixty-one.* But I'm determined not to react. Still, every missed call and unanswered text message is a reminder of their betrayal.

Their attempt to "help" cut me deeply — a wound in my soul that is becoming more and more painful with time. I can't stop replaying the situation over and over again. How did I not see it? How did they know I would reach out to Lulu? Do they really know me better than I know myself? Though the bigger question is whether I even know myself anymore.

I let my body settle into my office chair — facing the door, of course, as it's Tuesday — and smile into my lavender tea. *Savor the small things.* I tap my head, my temple, my collarbone. The practice soothes me, but I still jump at the sound of something scurrying across the windowsill. Or was it someone? My head snaps around and I scan the area out the window, expecting to see Nate standing there again. But there's no one.

Stop being so paranoid, Aisha, I remind myself, shaking my head. But it's certainly easier said than done. I return to my computer where the equation my colleague emailed me earlier beckons to me and I must oblige. The numbers fill the room with mathematical magic that only my work can provide. I feel at ease.

But any time I begin to feel comfort wash over me, something interrupts it, breaking the wave until the despair comes crashing back down on me. It's often the buzz of yet another message from Lulu or Noora, a feeling of eyes on the back of my head, or a reminder of Lulu's visit.

A tap on the skylight makes my stomach drop. I leap to my feet and look up. I'm greeted with another tap. Tap. Tap. Tip tap tip tap tip tap. The panic evaporates off my skin as I realize it's only rain drops. My feet pull me toward my organized bookshelves where a single title calls to me.

Big Magic.

The vibrant blue spine sends a cold chill down my spine and the image of Lulu running her hennaed fingers over this very book comes to mind. Has she read it before? Is that why she was drawn to it? *Big Magic* is essentially a novel-length permission slip to creatives, supporting messy, authentic courage over fear and self-doubt. I purchased it years ago based on the recommendation by a podcast host who touted the read as "beyond life changing." As soon as I read it, I tucked it into my bookshelf along with the terror it unearthed within me. But it definitely seems like Lulu's vibe.

My mind drifts back to her visit and the deep connection we felt, or at least I felt, followed by the painful truth revealed at the end. The cruel joke guised as help. I won't let myself be fooled like that again. I sigh as I turn from the shelf back to my desk. I'm confronted by more reminders of my sisters: a crystal that Lulu left, a small piece of charred wood, and the four red envelopes containing my sisters' fake tarot cards. This must stop. I can't move on with these tokens around.

I snatch all the items up in my hands and march into the kitchen. One by one, I let the reminders of Lulu fall into the trash bin. The rock falls heavy and takes the envelopes with it to the bottom of the bin. After I wash my hands and make my way back to my work, a rumble of thunder brings my attention to the window nearest to my front door.

It's open.

I rush toward the soaked sill, trying to remember if and when I opened it. My wet fingers find the edge of the frame and pull down, but they keep slipping. This window has a habit of jamming, but I can usually yank it with enough force that it gives way eventually. I position the soles of my palms on the wood and prepare to give a heave when I spot it. An envelope sitting against the side of the sill, almost flush with the wall.

I abandon my task to grab the red envelope. It's wet but I can tell it's sealed.

CHAPTER 30

(THEN)

It looks like Blue's Clues threw up in here. The room is covered in primary colors with big yellow pillows covering the patterned couch and laid out in the far corner, near all the books and toys. Normally I'd love the sunbursts painted on the walls and would probably wander around to touch each of them — they kinda look like they'd feel rough and I love different textures — but I can't unclench my muscles. It took all my strength to force my legs to move from the car to this room this morning. Now that I'm here, I can't seem to unclench my muscles. To be honest, the colors are making me a little nauseous. That and the bright lights shining down on me and the detective sitting across from me.

"Could you tell me what happened next?" he asks with a big smile on his face. He sure doesn't look much like a detective though. Instead of a suit or a uniform like investigators wear in the movies, this man is wearing jeans and a plaid shirt. He actually looks a bit like Paul Bunyan. How is Paul Bunyan going to help me? "After Kayla ran off?"

I give a couple of quick nods and tighten my grip on the pillow I'm holding against my chest. It feels good to hug it, but the longer I do, the more I wish it were Kayla instead of just a stupid pillow. A shiver goes through me as I think about Marie holding Kayla's lifeless body. All the life and joy had been pressed out of her. I squeeze the pillow in front of me even tighter. What I wouldn't give to have Kayla back right now.

Paul Bunyan clears his throat. "Whenever you're ready."

"Sure," it comes out as just a squeak and I try to focus on the detective's question. "Then I started looking for her. I followed the trail down to the river where we'd just come from, thinking maybe she went home."

"Good," he nods, keeping his eyes on me and that smile on his face. "Can you tell me what you did while you looked? Did you shout for her? Stop at any point? What did you see?"

"Yeah, of course, I called her name tons of times." Did he think I was an idiot? I wouldn't just abandon my best friend. I looked and looked for her, although it was too late.

"My calls echoed all down the river, so I knew she'd hear me if she were mad and just waiting, or whatever." My heart starts to beat faster at the thought. Did she hear me? Right before she died? I can't think about that right now. It's too sad, but the thought is there, and it won't let go. I shake my head, trying to get rid of it. All I wanted to do was find the spell book to protect my sister, but my best friend was the one who really needed protecting. And I failed. At both.

"What else did you do? See?"

I look down at the pillow, trying to push the thought aside

and remember what happened and in the order that it happened. "Um, I think I collected stones? Flat ones," I add. "For skipping."

"Mhmmm." This seems to pique his interest. "And, Aisha," he leans in slightly, his voice getting a little slower and quieter now, "did you use these stones to hit or throw at anything? Or anyone?"

My arms go slack and the pillow tumbles off my lap to the ground. "Omigod, no! Of course not!" My face starts to feel hot. What kinda question is that? "Do you think I hurt her or something?" I spit out.

"Oh no, Aisha," he leans back now, holding his hands up. "*I* don't think that at all." His emphasis on the "I" is very evident. Someone must then, why else would he ask that? But who? My heart beats faster as I try to wade through the fog in my mind to find the answer. One person finally rises to the surface: Dr. Wiley.

The detective continues, "We just want to make sure we cover all bases and do a full investigation before confirming that Kayla's death was an accident."

I nod my head but I'm only half listening. Dr. Wiley said he'd stay quiet. Well, he didn't say it, but he motioned to me that he was going to. The finger raised to his lips. It's a universal sign, isn't it? Did I misread things, or did he do it so he could throw me under the bus?

"How are you feeling?"

After a few minutes, I finally answer, "I don't know." It's all I can think to say, but it's truth. I'm not really feeling anything. I'm numb.

CHAPTER 31

(NOW)

I DON'T EVEN bother opening the envelope this time. Instead, I drop it right into my trash bin along with the others, then grab my phone and start dialing. Of course, she picks up on the first ring.

"I am so so happy to hear from you, Ish." Lulu's voice sounds breathy again, but more out of breath versus her wispy tarot voice.

"I'm not calling to check in," I say flatly. "Or hear your explanation. I just need you to stop sending the tarot cards." I'm too tired to pace around the kitchen — not physically, but emotionally exhausted. I let myself fall onto the couch and sit slumped over with elbows on knees. Lulu doesn't say anything for a moment, so I press my phone into my ear, assuming I just can't hear her. "Uh, Lu? You still there?"

Finally, she speaks. "You got another card?"

"Um, yeah." Why is she still playing this game? I'm on my feet now, walking to the kitchen. I peer into the trash bin just to make sure I'm not making it up. Nope, it's real and staring right back at me. "It just arrived at my door. Same way. Same creepy envelope." I hear her mumbling something away from the phone, like she's speaking to someone.

"Lu?" She's already put me through so much, the least she can do is just admit that they're still messing with me. I've spent the last few days in a continuous state of panic and paranoia, looking over my shoulder every few minutes to see if someone is following me.

One of them. The fact that it was them should put me at ease — at least it wasn't some random or malicious person who has been watching me for who knows how long. But it makes it even more unnerving to know that it was someone I know. Someone I trust and care about. Just as my thoughts swirl around in circles in my head, I find myself pulled into my pacing circle.

"Lu, are you still there?" The silence isn't helping.

"Yes, I'm here. Noora's here too."

I roll my eyes. I should have figured.

"It wasn't us, Ishie."

"Come again?" I stop in my tracks. *What the eff?*

"We didn't send it."

"Stop messing with me," I snap back. My heart races and I feel the heat rise up my chest and toward my ears. I've had more than enough of this.

"We're not." Noora is on the phone now, and the tremor in her voice leads me to believe that she's more panicked than even I am.

"Then who sent it, huh?" I demand. I squeeze the phone

a little tighter, my knuckles turning white as I wait for their answer. Two… three can play this game. There's more mumbling on the line — they're probably trying to get their next lie straight.

"We don't know," Lulu finally says. "We promise you, this wasn't us."

"How can I believe you after what you've done?" I try my best to keep my voice steady, but it audibly breaks. Noora must have snatched the phone back from Lulu because I hear her voice again.

"We never meant to hurt you and would do anything to repair the trust we've—" she starts, but I can't hear any more.

"Oh, stop it with the psychiatrist-speak, Sissy."

"I just—" Before Noora has a chance to finish her thought, I end the call.

I turn my phone off and slam it on the kitchen counter. How could they deny it when it's so obvious that they did this? Without thinking, I snatch the envelope out of the bin and rub the paper between my fingers. The paper is still soggy from the rain but I can tell it's that same woven material that looks like it's overpriced and way too fancy for a casual letter. *See, this has Lulu and Noora written all over it,* I confirm in my head. *And I'm sure the message is in the same personal, cryptic style as the others.* My finger dips into the opening at the edge of the envelope and moves along the top, ripping right at the seam. A perfect line.

I pull the card out and my throat tightens with unease. Something's not adding up here. There's something different about this tarot card. About the way it feels. I rub it between my fingers, and something flutters to the ground. I slowly hinge over and feel for the fallen object. Then the realization hits me.

This isn't from my sisters. My hand trembles as I reach for my cell and redial.

"Please come over," I breathe into the phone, keeping my eyes glued to the wilted tarot card. "I need your help. Now."

CHAPTER 32

(THEN)

I PICK UP my Trapper Keeper and place it back on the left side of my desk. I finally got a desk in my bedroom when I went into the 4th grade, but I didn't really use it much back then. But with 6th grade starting in just a week, I need to get all my supplies organized and ready for the school year. The pinks and yellows of the smiling tiger on the front of my Trapper Keeper match perfectly with my pink pencil case, but something about it being there just doesn't feel right. I grab it and put it down on the right side again. Not right here, either! I squeeze my hands into fists and try to figure out what's wrong, but nothing comes up in my brain. Nothing on my desk seems to be in the right order. Ever. Just as I reach down to open my desk drawer to toss the thick binder inside, Lulu skips into my room.

"Ishie!" she yells, jumping up and down on my bed. "Help

me with my dance routine!" The perfectly laid comforter and decorative smiley pillows bounce around with her. I jump off my chair and run over, trying to keep the pillows from falling onto the floor. If they do, I'll need to put them in my closet for five nights before I can arrange them back on my bed.

"Stop!" I push the pillows away from the edge and try my best to smooth the wrinkles on bed. "Lu, you can't do that!"

Her face falls and she sits still on the edge of the bed. "Sorry, Ishie, but remember you said you'd help me?" Lulu's big watery eyes look up at mine and remind me. I did say that.

A few weeks ago, when we'd learned about dance team tryouts for the new school year, I excitedly urged her to think about trying out. "But you are such a good dancer!" I'd said when she protested. "You can jump super high and are so graceful. Even Preetie Auntie said so when we danced at her Diwali party that one time!" Lulu's face lit up when I said I'd help her with her audition routine, but now the light has completely dimmed.

That was before the night at the river. Now everything is completely different.

"I just have a lot to do," I explain to my little sister as I work to get my bed back to its perfect state. After that I need to figure out my desk setup, *then* finish my summer reading list. I just won't be able to focus on the words until I know everything is in its place on my desk. And my bed. And my closet. A few other items are sitting in there waiting for their five days to be up before I can put them back out.

"Can we do it tomorrow?"

Lulu plops off the bed and stomps her feet. "But the auditions are tomorrow."

"I know, I know." I squeeze my eyes shut and count the hours left before bedtime. I have less than six hours to get all this done. *Six hours. Six. Six. Six times six is thirty-six.* My hair sways back and forth as I shake my head. *OK, better.* But the longer Lulu is in my room, the more I'll need to do to make everything just right again. My pillows, comforter, closet, and desk.

"I'm so sorry, Lu. I really am."

Her eyes overflow with tears as she walks toward the door, her feet dragging along the shag carpet.

"You never have time for me anymore," she sobs, then slams my door.

I turn back to my desk and grab everything off it, placing it all in a drawer, closing it, then starting from scratch. I need to get this right. A big sigh is pushed out of my lungs by the guilt that starts to take over my body. Deep down, I know it's not my desk that's the problem. It's me. I just don't know what's broken inside my brain or how I can fix it.

*   *   *

When I get home from the library the next day, Lulu isn't tumbling across the living room floor or playing with her Easy-Bake Oven.

"Lu!" I call as I hang my backpack up on the back of my bedroom door. Then I hear it. Sobs coming from her room. My heart sinks as I remember what today was: her dance auditions.

Mom's muffled footsteps are right outside my door, but before I can even ask her what happened, the look on her face gives me my answer. Lulu didn't make the team.

Mom crosses her arms and tilts her head to the side as she lets out her breath. I can see red pen marks on her chin and the collar of her shirt. Her eyes wear the same red shade; a reminder that she's working hard for us, even if we don't always see her.

"She needed you, Aisha," is all Mom says before walking back to her lesson plan.

When I see Lulu at the dinner table, she says it's fine and that she didn't even want to be on the team, but I know it's not fine. None of this is fine, and I'm not sure if it ever will be.

CHAPTER 33

(NOW)

LULU PRANCES RIGHT through my door as soon as I open it —
without taking her shoes off, though I let it slide because I'm
so wound up; we have bigger fish to fry — but Noora hesitates
at the entrance. Instead of the pant suit she was wearing the
other day, she's wearing cream-colored linen pants and a cham-
bray shirt. A little more relaxed, but still impeccably put together. I wouldn't expect anything else from my big sissy. Her
eyes gleam with curiosity as she peers around the living room.
I wonder what is going through her mind right now. Does she
regret never reaching out to me despite being in the same town
for most of our adult lives?

But we skip the niceties and I hand them the tarot card
immediately.

Lulu's eyes widen as she takes it in. "We didn't send this," she whispers, looking into my eyes with a mixture of concern and confusion. I believe her, and I need her help now more than ever to figure out who exactly this card is from.

"This is bad."

"What does it mean?" My shoulders tighten with the weight of her statement. I've watched enough of her YouTube and Instagram videos to know that my sister can easily spin things to reveal their silver lining. Every one of her readings has a positive message, so the fact that she's so panicked about this particular card — and the situation altogether — makes me even more unsettled.

"OK, so this is The Tower card, see?" She begins explaining the card to us and we listen intently from our posts — me pacing behind the couch and Noora still standing by the front door. The image on the card shows a tower engulfed in flames and figures falling headfirst from the top of the building.

"The Tower represents chaos. Destruction." A chill runs through me. Yes, this is very very bad. "Things are about to change, and quickly," Lulu continues. "Usually when I pull this card for someone, it's a sign to surrender to the havoc. Trying to control things will only make them worse."

"And this card has a handwritten message, just like the others," Lulu explains to Noora, who nods but remains silent.

"'As the Tower crumbles in a sudden collapse, veiled truths are revealed. Speak them first, or brace for chaos.' Whoa, that's cryptic. Were ours that creepy?" She isn't speaking to me though; she's asking Noora, who just shrugs and remains silent, her body folding inward as if she wishes she could disappear into the wall.

"Uh, I think I'm probably the best person to answer that, and yes," I interject, putting a significant amount of emphasis on the "yes," "they were definitely that creepy." What secret could this card be referring to? It cautions to speak it before anything else, but how can I if I have no idea what truth it's referring to?

Lulu flips the card over, running her fingertips over the details on the back. Instead of the intricate design on the backs of the other tarot cards, this one is a pale blue plaid. The pattern looks incredibly out of place next to the whimsical and eerie illustration on the other side. "Tarotee," she murmurs.

"Hmm?" Noora and I look to each other then back at Lulu, who falls onto the couch with her eyes still fixed on the card.

"It's a textile pattern that was eventually used as the back pattern for the Rider-Waite-Smith tarot deck." Lulu looks to me as if she's expecting some kind of reaction, but I have none. Her words mean absolutely nothing to me. "Like, the OG tarot deck? Arguably the most iconic iteration of all?" Nope. I shake my head.

"Well, this pattern has kinda become the standard for the deck. Even though, fun fact—" She sits up straight and flaps the card around excitedly. The smile on her face tells me that she's really passionate about this. "—the original Rider-Waite-Smith created in 1909 actually had a solid blue back." Lulu looks at us expectingly.

"You're not doing a good job at convincing Aisha that it wasn't us, Lu." Noora sighs and finally moves away from to the door to sit down next to her on the couch. I take the spot on the other side of Lulu. As we sit in my living room, huddled together looking at the card, it feels comforting — exactly as it did when we were children. I find myself caught between the warmth of having my sisters close by and the chilling situation we're in.

"No, I believe that it wasn't you," I break the comforting silence and touch my front pocket. My knee won't stop jiggling up and down, shaking the entire couch, though my sisters don't seem to mind. But I haven't told them everything. I want to feel safe and trust them entirely, but can I?

"Because of the different pattern on the back." Lulu delivers it as a statement rather than a question, though she's absolutely wrong. I would have expected my sisters to send different cards to make it look like it was a copycat sender rather than them. So no, that's not what tipped me off.

"No, because of this." I stand and reach into my front pocket and present Lulu with the other items I found in the red envelope. She gasps and hands them to Noora, who looks equally spooked.

We need to figure out who did this.

CHAPTER 34

(NOW)

"Why didn't you lead with this?" Lulu shouts at me as she paces around the living room. Her effortlessly tousled appearance is now a proper mess — my sister's denim corset top is askew with one strap twisted around itself, and her lavender eye shadow is smeared under one eye. I've never seen her so spooked and willing to look less than her best. "Th-this is way more important than the card."

Noora has the items now, holding the torn paper by the edge as if it could jump out and bite her at any moment. It's not just any scrap, it's from a page in our spell book, the one we had as children. The torn and now water-warped paper reads "Fluttering Heart Charm to Catch Your Crush's Eye."

The wrinkles in Noora's forehead right now tell me that her mind is going a million miles a minute.

"Aisha…" she starts, but her voice trails off. "This is why we sent you the cards."

My body instinctively jerks backward. What do they know? This doesn't make sense. I point to the spot on the couch next to Noora and look right at Lulu. "Sit." Then back to Noora. "Explain."

My mind spins as they recount the last several weeks. It began when Lulu received a threatening and incoherent letter to her PO box. "Unfortunately, stuff like this happens all the time with influencers," she explains. "That's why I list a PO box on my website instead of a physical address." The letters kept coming, though, and became more and more personal. When one mentioned my name, not just A. Wren but Aisha, that's when Lulu started to get worried. But when they began arriving at her house and made mentions of revenge, she really panicked.

Lulu keeps her real identity close to her chest, just as I do, so the fact that someone knew things beyond her Lumaara alter ego suggested that this was more than just a crazed fan — this person could potentially be dangerous. She looped Noora in immediately who helped concoct this plan.

"That's why we needed to reenter your life, Ish," Noora says quietly. "We know the way we went about it was cruel, but we were worried you'd shut us out again if we didn't do it this way."

My eyebrows shoot up at her statement. I can't believe this. "Shut *you* out?" My temperature starts to rise as I reflect on the last two decades. Noora moving into the dorms early then abandoning the family entirely. Lulu focusing all her energy on drama. And me holding this secret for so long. All three of us tried our best to be pleasant and cordial around each other, but it was all superficial. Surface level. We never had deep conversations or talked about that night again.

I know I wasn't the best big sister I could have been — I let a lot of things fall through the cracks — but the blame for our disconnection isn't all on me.

"You were just so wrapped up in all of your… stuff," Noora says, moving her hands in a wide circle to indicate what this "stuff" could be, but I know. My counting, anxiety, and OCD. Her acknowledging my struggles feels validating, but it also stirs up a deep sadness within me. Sorrow that she noticed and did absolutely nothing.

"Well, you could have helped me." I keep my eyes on the coffee table between us. I can't bring myself to meet my sister's eyes. It seems so silly bringing it up now, but it's something I've held onto for years.

"Ish, I was a teenager. I could barely take care of myself," Noora says, shifting her weight on the couch and clasping her hands together. "I just wanted to get away from it all. I'm sorry I didn't go about this the right way."

"I just felt so alone then," I sigh. "And I still do." The stillness in the room vibrates around us. Not only have I felt alone, but I thought I was alone all this time. The notion that someone was watching me nearly caused me to spiral, but the truth is that someone *has* been watching over me. And my sisters were somehow trying to protect me, even in this cruel way.

"There's no need to point fingers, Sissies. We're in this together now." Lulu breaks the silence with her cheery upbeat voice, meanwhile she pops off the couch and grabs Noora's hands to pull her to a standing position, too. She tries to get us to embrace in a group hug, but it just feels like an awkward huddle, our arms unnaturally trapped by our sides and our cheeks squished together.

"That sounds like a High School Musical song, Lu," Noora mumbles from behind a curtain of Lulu's thick hair.

"Aish," Noora says, releasing her grip on us, "what about this other one?" She holds up the other wrinkled paper I'd handed her along with the spell page. It's the same size as a tarot card.

"Do you recognize that pattern?" I point to the delicate swirls and dots strategically placed over the piece of paper. The emerald color is slightly muted due to the rain, but I recognized it almost immediately. I'm not sure my sister does, though.

"No," Noora says at the same time as Lulu shouts, "Yes!" She leaps to her feet and grabs it out of Noora's hands to examine it more closely.

"It's my tarot deck!" Lulu runs her fingers over the pattern. "I got it in Turkey during a backpacking trip years ago." Her voice becomes quiet and she narrows her eyes at the card. "It's a really rare deck. I haven't seen anything like it before."

"What does it mean?" Noora asks.

This time my sisters look to me for answers. "It was glued onto the back of the tarot card," I explain. "The only reason I noticed it was because the entire envelope got wet and the fake back page started to curl up."

Lulu's mouth drops open.

"Wait," Noora says, looking between the two of us. "I still don't get it."

"Someone printed out the exact pattern of the deck we sent to Aisha in order to mimic our cards." Lulu says it in almost a whisper. Her eyes don't leave the piece of paper sitting in her hands.

"Someone's been watching *all* of us."

CHAPTER 35

(THEN)

I JOLT AWAKE, sitting up so fast I have to take one hand off my chest and use it to grab onto my twin bed frame to keep from falling off. My nightie sticks to my skin. Both are totally drenched in cold sweat, and so is my hair. Pieces stick to my forehead and cheeks, just like the way they were on Kayla's face that night. The way they just were in my dream. My heart is racing, and my lungs are going so fast I don't feel like I'll ever catch my breath.

"I can't breathe!" I'd whispered to Mom the first time it happened. I had woken up in such a panic that I'd been sure I was having a heart attack. "My lungs," I'd gasped. "My heart. It's going to beat out of my chest." Mom carried me back to my bed, stroking my hair to try to calm me.

"You're OK," she told me. "It was only a nightmare. Just

breathe in and out." I followed her instructions, but nothing felt like it would be OK.

Was I going to feel like this forever? I couldn't remember the dream, but my body couldn't shake the feelings of dread or panic. Even after an hour, the pit of worry was still there in my belly. Like after you swallow a watermelon seed and know it's just sitting there in your stomach. But Mom didn't leave. She whispered stories about unicorns and kittens into my ear and rubbed my back until I fell asleep.

That was just the first of many episodes, and Mom's patience wore a little thinner with each one. She said I could wake her up any time I had a nightmare, but I could see the exhaustion in her eyes. She'd yawn as she made breakfast in the morning and then brew another pot of coffee as soon as she finished the first.

Most of the time, it's just better for everyone if I don't even tell her. I try to steady my breath by myself by breathing in deeply, then letting it all go like she showed me. Breathe in. Breathe out. When I close my eyes, I see little wisps of the dream. They're becoming more vivid. Always the same place — the Rio Grande — but some details change. Sometimes I can fly. Other times, I can only move in slow motion. But in this dream, I'm the one in the water.

I feel Dr. Wiley's hands on my wrists as he drags my body to shore. I try to help him by getting to my feet, but it's useless. I can't move any part of my body. *I'm alive*, I want to yell, but my mouth won't move. He brings his head to my chest to listen for breathing and feels for a pulse, just like he did with Kayla. If I'm in the water, where is Kayla? I blink really quickly, trying to communicate something. Anything.

As my eyes move side to side, I see a glimpse of blue. My stomach does a flip, and I feel a cloud of dread sit over me.

Someone is following us. Dr. Wiley starts rhythmically pressing on my chest, and the dread gets so much stronger that it's almost overwhelming. *Help*, I try to scream through the cloud. In what feels like a split second, Kayla is beside him, kneeling down with her blue shirt hanging over me. Sissy? It was you hiding in the salt cedar? I'm shocked but also happy to see her. *Sissy, I'm in here! Help me.*

She looks right into my eyes with an evil smile. "No, don't save her," she says to Dr. Wiley. "She didn't save me. Leave her." My breath gets caught in the inside of my throat. Did I fail to save her?

The image of Kayla leering over me sticks in my mind even after my breathing slows down. It felt so real, and I can't seem to shake the lingering feelings of guilt.

I peel my damp nightie off before the chills can set in and drape it over my nightstand. My sheets feel good against my clammy skin. My body is exhausted but my mind won't rest. *One sheep, two sheep, three sheep.* I try the trick Granny showed me to fall asleep the first time I slept over at her house. It worked wonders, but I haven't needed to use it since then. *Four sheep, five sheep. Five, five, five, five.* The number feels stuck to my brain, but it feels good to repeat it.

Five, five, five times five is twenty-five. Twenty-five by twenty-five is six hundred and twenty-five. The multiplication tables float around my skull and calm my racing thoughts.

CHAPTER 36

(NOW)

NOORA IS ONE step ahead of us with a legal pad already splayed across her lap, her eyebrows knotted in concentration. The pen in her hand flies across the page in quick, staccato motions as she fills the page with name after name of possible suspects. Though I can't read what she's written down from across the room, I can see that she's listed at least a dozen or so — but I can't fathom how. In my mind, only one or two people could have done this.

"Well, we've already ruled out Dr. Wiley, " I offer. "Who would otherwise be at the top of my suspect list. " I look to my sisters, who seem to share a sideways look. Lulu's eyes dart to Noora then down to her hands, her long hair falling over half of her face.

"Wait, what was that look? "

"Lu…" Noora prods.

The deceit hangs heavy in the air. What is going on?

"You did talk to him, right? " I ask. When we FaceTimed the other morning, Lulu was outside Dr. Wiley's house. I recognized his lush, green lawn right away. She said that she'd spoken to him, didn't she? That it wasn't him? I start to replay the conversation in my head, trying to figure out if I misheard things. Maybe I'm misremembering.

My hands twist and grasp each other firmly as I watch the memory play across my mind like a movie until a realization interrupts it. That was when Lulu and Noora were sending the cards, I recall with a little shake of my head. Of course, she didn't speak to him. She had no reason to believe he was sending the cards because she was.

Lulu confirms my suspicions with a head shake. "No, I didn't, " she squeaks. My lips purse together.

"But it could be him now, " Noora adds. With this card. "

I shift my weight as I try to mentally fit the puzzle pieces together. Even after all these years, I'm still unsure whether Dr. Wiley is the good guy or the bad guy. He tried to save Kayla when I couldn't, but did he tell the police that I was somehow involved in her death? I want to talk things through with my sisters and share the truth with them — finally tell them what happened that night — but the words are caught in my throat.

"I think it's definitely a possibility, " Lulu says. "Right, Ish?"

They both stare at me expectedly. Now would be the time to tell them everything, including the fact that I'm anything but a hero. I'm an imposter. It's the perfect opportunity.

"Mmhmm, " I mumble.

The bubble of solitude grows around me as my sisters discuss their plans to approach Dr. Wiley — for real this time. They'll take Noora's car and, after talking to Dr. Wiley, swing by her place, which just happens to be in our old neighborhood, to let her dog out. However, I can hardly hear them because I feel so far away, slipping back behind the veil of my isolation.

"You're coming with us, right?" Lulu pauses in front of me and motions to the open door. I've walked through that doorway only once in the past seven years, and it felt like stepping back into a past that I want to forget. I'm not sure if I have it in me to repeat it again, at least not so soon. Noora seems to read my face like a book.

"You've been through a lot the last several days, Ish." She pushes a flyaway back behind my ear. "Why don't you stay here and keep brainstorming possible leads." I'm grateful for the excuse to stay and for the compassion my big sister is showing me. But her next words catch me off guard.

"And when we get back, I'll get you a referral for someone who can talk to you about treatment. For your OCD." A mix of relief and humiliation washes over me as she gives my shoulder a squeeze.

"Thanks, " I say in a voice just above a whisper, avoiding eye contact as she disappears into the bright sun.

After I turn all four locks behind them, I collect the legal pad from the coffee table and begin tidying up. Working through the list and brainstorming while my sisters are out will allow me to contribute, at least a little bit. The shame of staying behind gnaws at my insides, but I push it aside. I need to help in any way that I can.

"I could use some hummingbird magic right about now," I mumble to myself as I straighten the throw blanket resting across the arm of the sofa. I hope Blaze is around, though I'm sure she will be. She always knows when I need her.

A faint smile tugs at my lips as I walk into my office. The familiar scent of books mixed with lavender and Lysol fills my lungs as hope fills my heart. Being surrounded by all my favorite things instantly slows my racing thoughts. And my heart rate and respirations return to an almost-normal pace. Like a weight as been lifted. Despite what's going on outside these walls — my sisters' sudden return, the copycat stalker, and Dr. Wiley's involvement — I feel safe here.

But the warm feeling evaporates off my skin as soon as I reach my desk. Right there on my keyboard sits a splash of red.

Another envelope.

CHAPTER 37

(NOW)

THEY CAME INTO my house. My safe space. How did they get in? When did they do it? I slowly turn my head, scanning my seemingly empty office. The sun casts long shadows across the hardwood floor, and even the branches outside seem to stand still for me. There's not a single movement or noise to suggest an intruder, but that doesn't mean they're not still here. My heart beats against my ribs and my breath quickens. *Just breathe, Aisha.*

I stand frozen for a moment, trying to devise a plan. I need to get out of here. It's not safe in my home, but the thought of standing out on the street with someone potentially following me out there sounds even more terrifying.

The casita! The idea slaps me in the face like a gust of frigid air.

I move slowly toward the back door, the creak of the floorboards echoing throughout the house. Still, I keep my steps deliberate and quiet. My clammy hands grip the envelope as I take another step. And another. And another. Until I'm finally flush against the back door staring out the doorlight at my casita. It looms in the distance like a forgotten dream.

Like many New Mexican homes, I have a little single-unit structure in my backyard that's detached from the main house. At one point, I'd considered turning it into a library or renting it out on Airbnb, but my agoraphobia has prevented me from visiting it in years. It's probably full of spider webs and mouse droppings.

My sweaty hand slips as I turn the doorknob. Who knows what the interior of the casita looks like now? I'm about to find out.

The door clicks shut behind me. I take a peek out the peephole to confirm no one followed me out here, then let my back glide down the door to the floor. Once my eyes have adjusted to the dark — the window shades are drawn and will stay that way as I don't want anyone to know I'm in here, least of all the copycat tarot card sender — I can see the interior. Sheets of plastic cover the mint green furniture that I'd chosen to compliment the sienna walls, though you can hardly make out either color through the dust. The couch looks dull gray rather than the vibrant shade I'd been so excited about. It feels akin to looking in the mirror.

But there's no time for introspection. Now that I've steadied my breath, I must call Lulu and Noora.

Neither of them answers. They're probably talking to Dr. Wiley, so I leave them each a quiet yet desperate message urging them to call me back ASAP. Then I tear into the envelope. But I don't even get past the back of the tarot card before I start to panic again.

Blue.

The entire back of the card is solid blue.

I close my eyes and grip my hands tighter and tighter. All I can see is the flash of blue from that night. It drags me back to the edge of the Rio Grande — the cold air stings my skin and my nose wrinkles at the sharp scent of salt cedar. A cascade of chills work their way down my spine at the visceral memory.

It has to be them. The stalker from that night and my copycat card sender are one and the same.

My phone vibrates in my back pocket with a text notification. It's Lulu. Finally.

Lulu: all ok??

Lulu: can't talk atm but we'll be back soon and tell you everything

Aisha: LU! 911 EMERGENCY!!!!

Aisha: Another card! This time IN MY HOUSE!!!

I send her a photo of it. This card features a man holding swords, and there are three, four, no, five swords in the image. *Five fives are twenty-five.* She responds with an onslaught of questions. After I assure her that I'm safely locked in the casita and she assures me that Noora is calling the police, her messages become calmer.

Aisha: What about the card though? What does it mean?

Lulu: it's the 5 of swords, ish

Aisha: Is that bad?

Lulu: it's definitely not good...

Lulu: wait is it upright or reversed?

What does she mean, upright or reversed? The card can be either depending on how you hold it. I'm looking at it with the image upright right now, but if I flip it, it's reversed.

Aisha: I don't know what you mean?

A tap on the window causes my entire body to jerk forward, sending my phone sliding across the floor. I hold my breath and stare at the trail it leaves behind — a clean slice of floor amongst the thick layer of dust. Has the stalker found me? My phone illuminates with another text from Lulu. Dust particles dance around in the light as if they're ecstatic to finally be free, then settle back with their friends on the ground. The casita remains eerily silent. After several minutes of listening, watching, and steadying my breath, I rise to peek out the window, then retrieve my phone.

Lulu: this is really important ish, they have different meanings depending on which way they're oriented. Try to remember how it looked when you took it out of the envelope?

My trembling fingers spin the card around and around, viewing it from every possible angle. I wrack my brain trying to remember that detail, but I can't seem to reach into the chaos of my mind to find it. My jaw aches from frustration.

Lulu: the writing!

Aisha: Oh yeah! It says "In the sword's reflection, hidden grudges fester and debts remain unpaid. All is not forgotten."

Lulu: whoa, super creepy, but I mean what way is the writing facing? Can you read it when the card is upright or reversed?

Ooooooh. I take a look at the card and turn it a few times before I can make out the small writing. It's only legible when the card is upside down.

Aisha: Reversed!

Lulu: shit, that's what I was afraid of

Aisha: What does it mean?

Lulu: conflict and reopening old wounds

Aisha: Yikes

Lulu: but in a word, I usually see it as meaning revenge

My heart drops. Revenge. The word digs at old wounds that still haven't healed. Who would want to get revenge? My mind keeps going back to Dr. Wiley. I don't think he'd have any reason to hurt me, but he did seem to do some obscure and unexplainable things, so it's possible he's the one who sent these cards. Plus, he certainly could have taken the spell book that night. Though there's one other person who knew about the spell book.

Another sound outside the door brings my attention back to the present. I'm still in danger here alone on my own property, and I worry my sisters might be in danger, too. The fear remains, but it's now intermingled with a fierce determination. The only practical thing to do is to seek them out. I'm not exactly sure where they are, but I'll find them. I just hope I can do it before the copycat stalker finds me first.

CHAPTER 38

(THEN)

DR. FRANCES, FRANKIE as she keeps asking me to call her, looks down at the blue gel pen still sitting in the pencil case. "What does that color bring up for you, Aisha?"

I just shrug and keep coloring in the swirly cat picture in front of me. There are thirty-three sections of the cat and I can't use one color more than the others, which is why I chose the green, yellow, and purple pens. The final picture will have eleven sections of each color. *Eleven elevens are one hundred and twenty-one.*

"You don't know?" she asks when I stay quiet. It's not that I don't like blue. The sparkly gel pen is actually a super pretty blueish teal color, but it reminds me of that night.

"It's just too sad."

Frankie's eyebrows uncross and she smiles at me. "It's un-

179

derstandable to associate blue with sadness. We don't say 'I'm feeling blue' for nothing."

I nod along with her, but that's not it. Every time I close my eyes I see the blue water of the river, the flash of blue following us, my fingertips turning blue because of the cold. Frankie should know this, shouldn't she? My parents are paying her to help me "work through the trauma" from that night. This is our fifth session in only a week. *Five multiplied by five is twenty-five, then squared again is six hundred and twenty-five.* They must have told her everything that happened by now. All I want is to push all the fog in my brain aside and figure out why this happened. Why Kayla? And why not me?

Frankie leans back in her big cushy chair and crosses her legs. She looks at the gel pens on the glass coffee table between us, scribbles something down in her notebook, then turns her focus back to me. "Are things any better with your sisters, Aisha?"

"No," I say as I color the cat's tail, pressing into the paper as I think about Lulu and Noora. Before I know it, my pen rips right through the paper. "Oh no!" I snatch the paper up and try to press the rip flat between my palms. "Do you have tape? We need to fix this," I cry to Frankie, who is staring at me. She doesn't respond and instead starts writing again in her notebook. "Please, hurry! We need to fix it." Tears flow down my face and splatter on the beautiful cat picture. "It's all my fault."

"Aisha," Frankie puts her hand on my knee and I stop jiggling it for a second, "it is not your fault." She says it with no more force than her other words. "She wasn't moving when you found her. You pulled her out. You did CPR on her. You did everything you c—"

"I know." I stop her because I just can't hear her go on, repeating my lies. "Kayla's death is not my fault. I did all I could."

I repeat the mantra Frankie taught me during our first meeting. My hope was that the more I said it, the more I'd believe it. But it feels as untrue now as it did a week ago. *Seven days. Seven sevens are forty-nine. Two thousand, four hundred and one. Better.*

"Good girl." She nods. "Now let's leave the page as is without feeling the need to fix it."

I nod, too, but when she looks down at her notebook, I place a gel pen over the rip. Maybe if I don't see it, I won't worry about it? It could work. Kinda like a Band-Aid. Not quite as sticky — the tape would have been way better, but at least I can't see the rip now.

Frankie taps the back of her pen on her notepad. "You were just telling me that things haven't improved with your sisters. They're still being distant?"

"Yeah." The word comes out of my mouth, but my mind is somewhere else. I can't stop thinking about the torn paper. I can't see it, but I know it's there. I squeeze my hands together, rubbing my knuckles with my thumbs. *Don't look. Just don't look at it.* Instead, I force my eyes over to the window in Frankie's office. We're in a part of Rio Erizo I've never been to. In place of the big trees and wildlife I see outside our windows at home, all I can see are buildings.

"Noora got permission to move into her dorm early, so she's been wrapped up in packing up her room and summer reading for her classes. I guess she couldn't wait to get away." I shrug as I say it, though I totally get it. If I could escape from all this pain, fear, and guilt, I would too. Noora gets to start fresh in college. A pang of jealousy hits me. "And Lulu is just in her own little world."

"I imagine it's really challenging having the two people you love most in the world become strangers overnight," Frankie says, then adds, "But just know everyone grieves differently."

I nod, though there are two other people I love with all my heart that I can't talk to anymore either.

"I miss them so much," I whisper, my head hanging over the table. Tears fall onto the cat again, causing the colors to bleed and blend into a wet vortex on the page.

CHAPTER 39

(NOW)

IRIS IS JUST as cheery this time as the first time she picked me up. "Well, long time no see!" she says as soon as I climb into her back seat. She doesn't seem to notice my lack of shoes, though I'm acutely aware. Every ridge and pebble in the path to her Uber pressed into my soles – I couldn't risk reentering my home for a pair of shoes. So, socked feet it is.

My heart is pounding, but Iris' smiling eyes are a welcome sight that puts me at ease immediately. I'm out of my home and getting as far away from the copycat as I can get, though my nerves continue to buzz under the cloak of comfort.

Iris opens her door and begins to step out, but I stop her.

"Oh, I'll get my own door this time." My heart is beating far more quickly than usual — my watch reports that my current heart rate is a whopping one hundred and nineteen beats per minute. *One hundred and nineteen; fourteen thousand, one hundred and sixty-one...*

Even though I've just been through this a few days before, it doesn't make it any less scary. And this time, I don't have a mask, gloves, backpack, or anything else as a security blanket. It's just me. I feel so vulnerable, I may as well be sitting here naked.

"You doing OK back there?" Iris' eyebrows turn up as she glances at me from the rear-view mirror.

I haven't stopped wringing my hands since I sat down. Her question pulls me out of my spiral of rumination, and when I look down, I see I've wrung a red welt in my hand. "Oh!" I jump.

"Darlin'?"

I shake my head as I shake out my trembling hands. "I'm OK, I'm OK," I say to myself more than to Iris.

"Would it be helpful if we chatted a bit to distract your mind?" Iris' offer sends a wave of calm over me.

"Yes, that would be incredible."

"Good!" I can't see Iris' face but I'm pretty sure she's smiling under her mask. "I'll start. Do you have anything fun planned today? Anything you can look forward to?"

I'd hoped I'd have a lot to look forward to with my sisters back in my life, but now all I have is more fear. Fear for their safety, fear that my house will never feel like a safe space again, and the looming fear that we won't figure out who the copycat stalker is and I'll need to live with the uncertainty that comes with that. I gaze out the window at the streets from my childhood dancing by and try to find a sense of calm.

"Nothing fun, I'm just hoping to find my sisters."

"I get it. What did you do to them?" Iris' voice is flat and low, a drastic contrast to her usual cheerful tone.

"Excuse me?" My stomach drops and a feeling of unease spreads through my belly.

Iris gives a hearty laugh. "Didn't mean anything by it, sweetheart. I was just curious what you did, if they ran off like this and you need to find them."

"I didn't do anything," I snap back. How does she know they ran off? I'd felt so comfortable with Iris initially that I'd waved off any feelings of distrust, but something's not adding up here.

"You sure, darlin'?" She raises an eyebrow and looks directly at me in the rear view. Iris' stare feels like it could burn a hole in my soul.

The panic blooms and spreads through my limbs. I feel a thought make its way to the forefront of my mind. *Open the door*, my mind urges me. *Open it and jump out.* Under usual circumstances I'd acknowledge the thought as anxiety, then move on, but this time it comes from a different place. From my gut. Something is very wrong and I need to get out of here. But could it just be anxiety? I squeeze my eyes shut and try to imagine a table where I can analyze the different origins. Was it a sudden thought? Yes. One tally in the anxiety column. Was there a tangible threat? Maybe. Was my fight or flight triggered? Definitely. More tallies.

I snap my eyes open. At this point all data points to anxiety, so I should just proceed as such. I plaster on a smile and try to make my voice sound upbeat, but my guise feels so thin and superficial that it could shatter at any moment. "Your accent is so unique, where are you from?"

"It's the 'darlin',' isn't it?" Iris laughs again. "I'm from East Texas, but I spent my early years right here. On this street, actually."

She says it so casually, but it feels like a dropped bomb. Rio

Erizo is a small community — I graduated from high school with less than 200 people in my class. Everyone knows everyone else's business, which can certainly be a bad thing, but it also made growing up here feel incredibly safe. Well, mostly safe.

"Your early years." I repeat what she said and let it sink in. I let my eyes wander over what I can see of Iris' face in the rear-view mirror and really look at her features this time. Initially I thought she was older, but she actually appears to be around my age, give or take a few years. I don't remember going to school with anyone named Iris, nor do I remember Noora or Lulu ever mentioning an Iris. Had we crossed paths? Between the large eyeglasses covering her face and the surgical mask, I don't recognize her.

"So did I," I say quietly. "Maybe we knew each other." Iris' vibrant purple hair has been freshly dyed since I saw her last, so there are no visible roots to determine her natural hair color, but if I had to guess, it could be a light or medium brown.

"Oh, we certainly did, darlin'. You know exactly who I am." Iris catches my eye again in the rear-view mirror and my heart sinks even further.

Her eyes. I didn't see it before, but they're like big chocolate kisses.

CHAPTER 40

(THEN)

DID THEY EVEN know her *at all?* I look around the school auditorium at everyone — students, parents, and teachers — in their black dress pants and tops, then scowl down at my own black overalls. I count fifteen rows by twenty-five seats on the main floor, packed with people dressed in her least-favorite color. That's a max of 375 drab people. *Three hundred and seventy-five multiplied by three hundred and seventy-five is... one hundred and forty thousand, six hundred and twenty-five.* Kayla would be so pissed if she saw us all wearing black. She loved colors — the brighter, the better.

"If you'll be seated, we'll begin momentarily." Principal Brown speaks into the microphone on the stage, which is littered with all kinds of bouquets, stuffed animals, and photos of Kayla. It's been five long weeks since that awful night, and I keep hoping someone will say something that'll help me make sense of it all. My fingers and toes are crossed that this ceremony will give me the answers I need.

I spot Lulu sitting with her class on the main audience level. I'd thought about finding her earlier so we could sit together and hold hands, but I knew she was still mad at me about her dance auditions. Plus, she seemed happy with the new friends she'd already made in drama club during this first week of school. So, I'm sitting alone on the far side of the balcony.

People have been talking about what happened to Kayla and rumors are already circulating, including a story about me fighting La Llorona to get Kayla's body back after the ghost pulled her under the water like she'd done with her own children. The things they whispered hurt. "What do you think La Llorona's spirit looks like?" "Did she hear her scream?" "Why didn't La Llorona drown Aisha instead?" I didn't want to deal with the hushed voices coming from the rest of my class, so sitting alone felt like the best option. For now, anyway.

I keep my eyes down on my lap, focusing on the red mark on my hand. The ink won't seem to come off no matter how much I rub it. On the way into the auditorium, I'd signed the memorial guest book. My hand shook as I scribbled my message with a red pen — the only one I could find that wasn't blue. It felt weird to write "Kayla" and I didn't want to sign my own name because I didn't really want anyone to know I was there. I settled on "I love you, Blaze." A little tribute to a nickname I called her every once in a while that represented the fiery personality that Kayla truly was.

Mr. Brown clears his throat and the chatter around the auditorium dies down. "We welcome everyone to Rio Erizo Middle School today to remember and celebrate the life of Kayla Perez. The last several weeks have been very difficult for our

tight-knit community, and we're grateful for the Perez's deci-
sion to wait until the school year to hold a service that allows
our entire school family to participate."

At the mention of Kayla's parents, Mr. Brown motions to
the left wing of the stage where they both stand. Even from up
here I can see that their eyes are red and glistening.

"Although Mr. and Mrs. Perez have relocated to our neigh-
boring state of Texas since Kayla's untimely passing, her memory will live on here in Rio Erizo. Please join me in a moment
of silence to begin our program."

During the service, I keep looking up at Kayla's parents.
They're hanging onto Mr. Brown's every last word, nodding as
he describes how smart, funny, and brilliant Kayla was. They
pat their eyes with tissue when he mentions the family — blood
and found — that she's leaves behind. When Mr. Brown says
my name, describing me as "the one who attempted to save her
beloved friend," I feel all eyes on my face.

But one pair burns through me with what feels like rage
instead of sadness.

Marie's.

She's up on stage with Kayla's parents. I haven't seen her
since that night. That awful night when it took the first re-
sponders hours to get Marie away from Kayla's body — she
refused to leave her. Anyone who came near would have to get
through her fists, shrieks, and clawing fingers first.

They'd moved to be with Mrs. Perez's family in Longview
the next week and I hadn't seen her since. And from the look
on her face, it's probably for the best that we haven't crossed
paths. If a bunch of EMTs and officers were scared of Marie,
there's no way I would have stood a chance against her, no
matter her size.

After the service, we gather on the school's football field

for a candlelight vigil. As the sun sets, the sky radiates with all sorts of bright colors: pinks, purples, yellows, and oranges. Now this is a tribute fit for Kayla. The slender white candles sway and bob as we pass along our flames. I turn to light the candle next to me and come face to face with Marie.

"H-Hi." I trip over my word, but she doesn't say anything. She just narrows her eyes at me, her mouth in a perfectly straight line.

"How are you doing?" I try again.

"How am I doing?" she hisses. "How do you think I'm doing?"

We're surrounded by people but no one seems to be paying attention to us. I hear sobs and sniffles coming from the crowd, but it feels like Marie and I are in our own little world. One I want to escape from ASAP.

"I'm so sorry, Marie." I look down and try to find the words to make things right, but I don't know what to say. As my eyes move down, I notice that Marie isn't wearing black like everyone else. Her dress is a deep blue color. I try to swallow the sense of dread that comes up but it's no use.

"Yeah, right," she says with an eye roll, interrupting my thoughts and bringing my eyes back onto her face. "Whatever."

Marie turns and walks into the crowd just as the vigil starts. Someone beside me mentions how beautiful the sea of candles looks against the fiery sunset, but all I can see is the blue of Marie's dress dancing in the breeze, mixing with the flash of blue that haunts my dreams.

CHAPTER 41

(NOW)

IRIS TEARS THE mask off her face and tosses it aside. Beneath the vibrant hair and fun glasses, I see it. I see *her*. Her facial features are much more angular, but there's no mistaking exactly who is in the driver's seat just inches away from me.

"Marie?"

I haven't uttered the name in years, and it feels heavy on my tongue. How did I miss all the signs? How did I not recognize her? It's been Marie all along.

"It's been a while, hasn't it?" Marie shoots me an evil smirk that makes my skin crawl.

My mind spins as I make sense of it all. The flash of blue, the tarot cards, the feeling of being watched. It was all Marie.

"*You* were watching me?" I swallow the truth, but it threatens to come right back up along with my lunch and an outpouring of questions: Why? For how long? How?

Marie cackles from the front seat as the car makes an errat-ic and violent swerve toward the median. My stomach drops. She's no longer the young girl I considered a sister for so long. Before me is a vengeful woman twisted by grief and rage — someone I need to get as far away from as I can. *Open the door,* my gut says again.

"Oh, it's so much more than that, darlin'," Marie sneers.

I catch a glimpse of her eyes in the rear view and recognize an animalistic expression, similar to the one I'd seen in her as she fought off the EMTs that night at the Rio Grande. Our car speeds up abruptly, then Marie slams on the brakes repeatedly, causing my seatbelt to bite into my shoulder. The screeching of the tires joins with her laughter to create a grisly symphony, which reverberates through my bones.

"I've been waiting for this moment for years, *Sissy.*" She says the word with disgust. "I heard everything that night. I heard Kayla confess her crush on you and you shut her down. After she fled, completely distraught, I lost sight of you both and didn't find you again until it was too late."

The vehicle lurches forward and I grip the door handle un-til my knuckles turn white. The venom in her voice is palpable.

"Until *after* you'd drowned my sister."

"No," I plead. "It wasn't like that at all."

It's all coming together. Marie's mood at the memorial. The odd questions by the investigator. But she has it completely wrong.

"I would never hurt Kayla." My voice is barely audible over the revving engine. Cacti and mountains are flying by us. We must be going at least 80, maybe 90 mph if I had to guess. Even if I could bring myself to open the car door right now, I'm not sure I'd survive a tumble onto the road at this speed. I continue trying to talk Marie down.

"It was an accident, Marie. You have to believe me."

"Lies!" she shouts and takes a sharp turn to the left. "You are a liar! You lied about everything!"

My heart leaps into my throat. She must know.

"Yes, I did lie," I begin, reaching a hand forward and placing it on the back of her seat right above her shoulder. Marie flinches and drives even more erratically. I bring my hand back. *OK, touch isn't a good thing here.*

"I lied about being the one to pull her out. Dr. Wiley did that, not me." My voice quivers as I speak, but I try my best to steady it. Maybe if I remain calm, she'll be calm, too, like with a dog, or a baby. "But I promise that's all I lied about. And I only did it because I was young and naive and thought that was what I was supposed to do."

An image of Kayla's lifeless body lying on the riverbank floats into my mind, but I don't shake my head or squeeze my eyes shut. I let it stay, just for a moment.

I sit with the sorrow and discomfort for longer than I have in years. I wish I could share the visuals with Marie so she could see exactly what I experienced and finally lay to rest this misconception she's lived with all these years, but it's no use. She only has my word, which she may or may not believe.

My phone buzzes in my pocket and I manage to glance at the message. It's Lulu.

Lulu: are you ok? Where are you??

I look out the window into the dusky night trying to catch a glimpse of any clues that could help me identify exactly where we are. We've been driving for a while now at high speeds, so I wouldn't be surprised if we're a few towns over by now, but the landscape outside looks incredibly familiar. I see the weeping willow, then Dr. Wiley's tire swing.

We're still very much in Rio Erizo. The peaceful streets are a stark contrast from the storm taking place within this metal box.

"How could you?" she shrieks again, making an abrupt stop that jolts us both forward.

Now is the time. I have to do it *now*. I feel the freeze creep through my body. If I don't act quickly, I'm going to be trapped here with Marie. While I know she's still processing the loss in a much different manner than I am, I'm not entirely sure what she's capable of. And I simply can't hang around to find out.

Don't think about it, just do it.

I count down, *three, two, one,* then open the door and jump into the unknown.

CHAPTER 42

(NOW)

THE PEBBLES DIG into my knees and palms as I scramble to the sidewalk, but I barely feel them. I just need to get away from her. I fling my body behind an electrical box just over the curb and strain my ears for Marie. It's possible she'll keep driving, but it's also possible that she'll come back for me.

She clearly wants revenge.

The sun has almost completely disappeared behind the Sangre de Cristo Mountains, leaving the range radiating an ominous red color — the blood of Christ. But if Marie catches up with me, it could be my blood staining these mountains.

I press my body up against the cool metal of the box and trace my fingers over its painted side. These utility boxes often have such fun and creative art painted on them, like aliens and UFOs, but this particular one happens to have a hummingbird design. A hummingbird with a red throat and huge, glorious wings. "Blaze," I whisper to it. *I can be strong.*

A crunching sound pulls me out of my reflection. It's not too far away, but even if I did peek out around the utility box, I don't think I could make out exactly what or who it is. There are so few streetlights in this neighborhood. I hold my breath and will my trembling body not to make any noise as the in-stinct to freeze begins to take over. But I can't let it. Not this time. Not ever again.

The five senses grounding practice come to mind, and I take a deep breath. What can I smell? My racing heart starts to slow a bit as the scent of approaching rain fills my nostrils. What can I hear? Feel? A few cicadas hum, and I feel the stick-iness of the blood from my scraped knee between my fingers. Each detail brings me closer to the present.

The approaching footsteps grow louder and louder and I know I need to move. Now.

I silently shift my weight, pressing my hand into the rough material of the box right over the painted bird's ruby chest in an attempt to summon some of Blaze's courage. Without a second thought, I lunge forward and run.

My breath comes out in short, ragged gasps. I taste blood and feel every jagged stone under my socked feet, but I keep pushing myself. *Don't look back.* The darkness envelopes me, helping keep me hidden from Marie, but I also have no idea where I'm going.

The sidewalk abruptly turns into packed dirt and my feet take an instinctual right turn. Though I can't see them through the shadows, my surroundings begin to feel familiar. Each turn and dip in the trail is like a distant memory, and I let my feet lead me down, farther and farther until I sink into soft sand.

The tree house.

I stop and allow my throbbing, socked feet to relish the cool ground. A sigh escapes my lips, but I'm quick to survey my surroundings. I can't hear Marie approaching or see anyone else. This small tree house used to be our sanctuary, but it feels more like a trap now. Still, I don't have much choice. It's either go up and risk walking into an ambush or keep running and risk being caught.

It takes me far fewer strides now to reach the decrepit house compared to my short adolescent legs. Old wood creaks and groans under my feet as I make the journey up toward our old hideaway. I duck inside the dark house and crouch against the wall, trying to catch my breath. The stale, musty air brings me right back to childhood, though it's so much more cramped than I remember. What I wouldn't give to return to the days when we played up here. When everything was simpler.

The sound of crunching branches pulls me back into the moment. I peek out the tree house doorway and see Marie's silhouette framed by the dimming colors of the sunset. Above her, a few bulbous clouds hang in the sky, their edges barely illuminated against the waxing moon before fading into the darkness.

"Oh Aisha, come out to play," she calls. "I know you're up there." Her voice has transformed back to Iris' buttery soft tone, though it has a new sickeningly sweet quality.

I squeeze my eyes shut and try to stay still, but it's too late. Marie's footsteps up the ladder echo through the wooden structure. One, two, three. *Three threes are nine. Nine by nine is eighty-one.* She's getting closer to the entrance. Panic fills me as I wrack my brain for what to do next.

My eyes search the dark tree house, but I see nothing. Even after a few seconds of letting my vision adjust, the small shack is pitch black. I squat down, feeling the old wood shudder and sigh with me, then grope my hands along the dusty floor. Maybe there's something I can use to defend myself? Anything that we might have left behind, or that our successors stored up here? My hand pauses on the cool floor when it occurs to me: even if I did find something use to as a weapon, could I bring myself to hurt Marie?

"You can run but you can't hide." Her voice taunts me, but I try to stay calm. Another thud of her foot on the ladder causes my heart rate to soar.

"Marie," I whisper, "you need to believe me. It was all an accident."

The climbing stops. Maybe my explanation is working. I try again, my voice picking up in speed and volume.

"She ran away and by the time I found her, she was already—" my voice breaks. "Gone," I finally finish the sentence.

My hand finds my chest as I realize I haven't entirely processed the loss and guilt around Kayla's death. Whenever emotions and memories come up, I stuff them back down, distracting myself with numbers. It feels different to actually *feel* what comes up.

"Are you sure?" Marie asks quietly.

"Yes!" I shift slightly and push myself up to a standing position.

She's beginning to understand. A flicker of hope lights my way and I take a small step toward the entrance, then another. Marie remains silent as I make my way to the warped door frame. When I finally poke my head around the corner and look down at my old friend, my blood turns to ice. She gazes up at me with an evil smirk.

"You really expect me to believe that?" she hisses, her eyes filled with rage. "You let her die!"

Marie lunges upward and her hand grazes my ankle. Fear

shoots through me like a jolt of electricity. Before I have time to react, the decrepit ladder gives way and her foot slips on the ladder rung and she's pulled downward.

"No!" I shout, reaching my hand forward, but it's too late. Marie falls backward and lands with a sickening thud. I squeeze my eyes shut and shake my head, trying to clear the image, but all I can see is the flash of terror across her face as she plummeted downward.

When I finally gather the strength to open my eyes and peer over the edge, preparing myself for the sight of her crumpled body, confusion washes over me. The ground around the tree house is bare, and a heavy silence rings in my ears.

Marie is nowhere to be seen.

EPILOGUE

Maybe stepping outside *will kill me, but maybe not. I'll never know, and that's OK.*

Each step I take feels like a victory. Healing isn't linear, but today definitely feels like a good day. My new therapist, Samantha, has explained that exposure and response prevention, or ERP, therapy is the gold standard treatment for my OCD. We started by exposing me to the mere idea of my biggest fears, including leaving my home and resisting the compulsion to count, as a technique to help reduce the associated anxiety response. Because I've been so diligent with my homework, we've graduated to the next phase.

I look down at my Chelsea boots. They're taking me farther away from my back door and closer to the patio furniture in the middle of the yard where Lulu waits for me and Noora with a pot of tea and handheld hummingbird feeders. A glance over my shoulder confirms that my big sister is just a few paces behind me. She flashes me an encouraging smile and waves, which give me a surge of confidence. One foot in front of the other.

Each of us is wearing a matching red apron. Red is far from my favorite color and has become quite a trigger for me ever since the cryptic envelopes. I'm working on not only addressing my fear of the color blue, but now red. Still, with each exposure, I'm becoming more and more confident.

Our blood red getups probably look hysterical and somewhat creepy from afar, and they're actually not part of an exposure exercise today. Instead, we're doing some hummingbird watching. They're attracted to this color and are more likely to approach when we wear red.

Still, Blaze will come feed from my hand even when I'm not wearing red. The more time I spend with her, the more I feel like maybe she is my Blaze.

As I walk forward, taking in the sight of the burgundy leaves and crisp sound they make under my feet, I feel my heart rate pick up a bit. I'm about a four right now. Samantha encouraged me to rate my anxiety level before and after doing exposures on a scale of one to ten. Another part of my therapy is resisting the compulsion to count. I just let the lone four hang there in the air without multiplying it. It feels so unnatural, but I want to get better. My lungs pull in a deep breath and the smell of roasting chiles wafts into my nose, making my stomach growl.

"Nate's been digging into this 'Iris' character," Lulu says. "Apparently, she was last seen waitressing in Glendenon, and he found a tagged photo of her on Instagram tattooing someone out of a shop in Ohio. But both leads have turned out to be dead ends." Lulu blows on her teacup and catches my eye.

Noora and Nate are determined to find Marie – Noora, to ensure that Marie gets the mental health help she needs to process her grief, and Nate, to protect Lulu from any danger. But I'd prefer to keep my distance. Fear has controlled my life for far too long, and I refuse to allow Marie to hold any more power over me.

Knowing that Marie is alive, and I wasn't unintentionally involved in her death — another death — puts my mind at ease. I'd rather focus my energy on the people who positively impact my life, like the two women right in front of me.

"Oh, is Nate here?" I ask, taking a final step and plopping down into a chair.

"No, I told him we needed some sister time."

I'm actually a little relieved. After getting to know my brother-in-law, I've determined that Nate is an amazing human and a perfect match for Lulu. He keeps her grounded by talking her out of elaborate, spontaneous plans — if only she'd shared the tarot card scheme with him, he would have shot it down immediately.

Even though I love spending time with him, it's nice to get some alone time with my sisters. The last several weeks have been a whirlwind of settling back into my regular life, but this time with both of them by my side. Lulu and Nate decided to stay in Rio Erizo, in my empty casita, for a while longer before heading back up to Colorado since they can work remotely, and Noora lives and works less than thirty minutes away from me.

All this time, my big sister has been so close.

When they'd visited Dr. Wiley, he revealed the truth about what happened that night by the river. I no longer have to carry a secret that felt like it might burn me alive. With my sisters' support, I'm working toward accepting that there was nothing I could have done to save Kayla.

"Why don't we take a look at those icebreaker questions you put together?" Lulu asks, placing a steaming cup of chai in front of me. The aromatic spices are just what I need to calm my nerves.

"Oh no, Ishie, you didn't!" Noora settles into the Adirondack chair beside me, giving me a playful slap.

I just roll my eyes. "Actually…" My hand reaches for my tea, and I take a long sip. The hot liquid hits my tongue then slides down my throat, warming me from the inside out. "I was thinking maybe we just talk."

My sisters look to each other, then back at me, both of them smiling.

"What do you two think about a sister trip next summer?" I ask.

"Somewhere tropical."

AUTHOR'S NOTE

Living with obsessive-compulsive disorder (OCD) can feel like throwing a Velcro ball at a furry wall – as soon as the intrusive fears come into contact with the brain, they're nearly impossible to pull away. Focusing on the thoughts in an attempt to untangle them usually just exacerbates the mess.

Writing a character that lives with OCD was incredibly important to me, not only to help break the stigma around mental health but to inform readers about the complexities of this condition. Obsessive-compulsive disorder is often misunderstood as being solely contamination fears or compulsive handwashing, but it can manifest in many ways, including existential obsessions, unwanted mental images, rumination, specific phobias, and counting compulsions – like those experienced by the protagonist of *Sisters Arcana*.

Research suggests that it can take anywhere from 12 to 17 years from the onset of symptoms to the time a person actually gets appropriate help for OCD. This range rings true for me, as 17 years passed between the time I first sat in therapist's chair and the time I received an accurate diagnosis. It took nearly that long for me to feel comfortable sharing my dark, unsettling thoughts.

I hope that sharing this story will help others feel less alone.

If you'd like to learn more about obsessive-compulsive disorder, the International OCD Foundation and NOCD offer valuable resources.

Remember: you are not your thoughts.

BONUS CHAPTER

While *Sisters Arcana* stands on its own, I felt compelled to write a bonus chapter from Kayla's perspective. This missing piece recounts the tragic incident on the Rio Grande through Kayla's eyes, offering a bittersweet clarity to the story. Simply scan the QR code below to download.

ACKNOWLEDGEMENTS

First and foremost, I want to thank you, dear reader, for giving this story a chance. The fact that you invested your valuable time in exploring grief, sisterhood, and OCD alongside Aisha means the world to me.

This book is dedicated to my sisters, Yasmeen and Sharifa, whom I admire more than anyone. Writing from the perspective of estranged sisters was a real challenge, as it's so unlike anything I've ever known. You two have been by my side through everything life has thrown at us, and I'm grateful that these experiences brought us closer together rather than tearing us apart.

To my forever first reader and husband, Aaron – you always have the greatest feedback. I will never stop staring at you while you read my work, eagerly awaiting your reactions to the twists.

I couldn't have brought this story to fruition without my Hedgie sisters of Quill & Cup. This book was entirely plotted, written, and edited during Prickles, and each of you who sat with me at the table played an important role in this journey. Thank you from the bottom of my heart for cheering me on through every milestone.

To my BFFs (Best Feedback Friends!) Amber and Courtney – thank you for reading the earliest iterations of this book. It wouldn't be what it is today without you.

Mommy and Daddy, thank you for encouraging me to chase my dreams, no matter how big or small. Nicole, you've helped me reignite my creative spark time and time again. Nikki, without your guidance, I never would have learned to hear my own intuition so clearly. Lisa, thank you for helping me refine a story that I truly love.

Of course, a writer is nothing without their writer's fuel (aka. coffee). Thank you, Little Bear Coffee, for keeping the caffeine flowing and providing a safe space for me to allow my ideas to flourish.

Movement is truly my favorite way to work through writer's block, and many plot holes were mentally repaired on the treadmills of Orangetheory Fitness – Albuquerque Midtown.

I'm not sure what I did to deserve so many incredible people in this lifetime, but I'm eternally grateful to everyone who has supported me on this journey.

ABOUT THE AUTHOR

Saleema Ishq is the best-selling and award-winning author of short thrillers, known for captivating readers with her unique blend of imaginative storytelling, suspense, and psychological tension. When she's not crafting stories — always with a cat curled up in her lap or walking across her keyboard — you can find Saleema coaching fitness classes, trail running in the Sandia Mountains, journaling, pulling tarot cards, or adding to her crystal collection.

Sisters Arcana marks her full-length novel debut.